THE B...
A proud, ...
S0-AGJ-753

Scandal has rocked the core of the infamous
Balfour family.

Its glittering, gorgeous daughters are in disgrace.

Banished from the Balfour mansion, they're sent to
the boldest, most magnificent men in the world to be
wedded, bedded…and tamed!

*And so begins a scandalous saga of dazzling
glamour and passionate surrender.*

**Each month, Harlequin Presents®
is delighted to bring you an exciting new
installment from THE BALFOUR BRIDES.
You won't want to miss out!**

MIA AND THE POWERFUL GREEK—
Michelle Reid

KAT AND THE DARE-DEVIL SPANIARD—
Sharon Kendrick

EMILY AND THE NOTORIOUS PRINCE—
India Grey

SOPHIE AND THE SCORCHING SICILIAN—
Kim Lawrence

ZOE AND THE TORMENTED TYCOON—
Kate Hewitt

ANNIE AND THE RED-HOT ITALIAN—
Carole Mortimer

BELLA AND THE MERCILESS SHEIKH—
Sarah Morgan

OLIVIA AND THE BILLIONAIRE CATTLE KING—
Margaret Way

Eight volumes to collect and treasure!

Kat stared up into icy black eyes which were skating over her with undisguised disapproval.

"You!" she accused, though her knees had turned to jelly and her heart was thundering so loudly that she felt quite faint. But what woman in the world wouldn't feel the same if confronted with that spectacular physique, clad in close-fitting black jeans and a soft white silk shirt—even if his handsome face was so cold that it might have been sculpted from some glittering piece of dark marble? "Carlos Guerrero!" she breathed.

"Who were you expecting?" challenged Carlos silkily. "It *is* my boat, after all."

Sharon Kendrick

KAT AND THE
DARE-DEVIL SPANIARD

The
Balfour
Brides

TORONTO • NEW YORK • LONDON
AMSTERDAM • PARIS • SYDNEY • HAMBURG
STOCKHOLM • ATHENS • TOKYO • MILAN • MADRID
PRAGUE • WARSAW • BUDAPEST • AUCKLAND

Special thanks and acknowledgment are given to Sharon Kendrick for her contribution to The Balfour Brides miniseries.

PLEASE RECYCLE · THIS PRODUCT IS RECYCLABLE

Recycling programs for this product may not exist in your area.

ISBN-13: 978-0-373-23704-3

KAT AND THE DARE-DEVIL SPANIARD

First North American Publication 2010.

Copyright © 2010 by Harlequin Books S.A.

To my Uncle Aidan—a great thinker, wit and musician—who could charm the birds from the trees. A great man all-round. I miss you.

All about the author...
Sharon Kendrick

When I was told off as a child for making up stories, little did I know that one day I'd earn my living by writing them!

To the horror of my parents I left school at sixteen and did a bewildering variety of jobs: I was a London DJ (in the now-trendy Primrose Hill), a decorator and a singer. After that I became a cook, a photographer and eventually, a nurse. I waitressed in the South of France, drove an ambulance in Australia, saw lots of beautiful sights but could never settle down. Everywhere I went I felt like a square peg—until one day I started writing again and then everything just fell into place. I felt like Cinderella must have done when the glass slipper fit!

Today, I have the best job in the world—writing passionate romances for Harlequin® Books. I like writing stories which are sexy and fast-paced, yet packed full of emotion, stories that readers will identify with, laugh and cry along with.

My interests are many and varied: chocolate and music, fresh flowers and bubble baths, films and cooking—and trying to keep my home from looking as if someone's burgled it! Simple pleasures—you can't beat them!

I live in Winchester, (one of the most stunning cities in the world—but don't take my word for it, come see for yourself!) and regularly visit London and Paris. Oh, and I love hearing from my readers all over the world...so I think it's over to you!

With warmest wishes,

Sharon Kendrick

www.sharonkendrick.com

CHAPTER ONE

EVEN the brilliant Mediterranean sunshine
couldn't lighten her mood.

With a stab of frustration, Kat pushed the
spill of dark hair away from her eyes and
leaned back against the soft leather seat of the
limousine. A week had passed, but the
memories of that night were still vivid. A
night when accusations—and counter-accu-
sations—had spun through the air like the
blade of a helicopter. And another guilty
family secret had reared its ugly head.

If only…

If only it hadn't happened at the glittering
Balfour Charity Ball—where half the world's
press had been camped outside, waiting for
an almighty scoop. Briefly, Kat closed her
eyes. Bet they couldn't believe their luck.

Last year's ball had been bad enough—when she had made a humiliating fool of herself in front of the arrogant Spaniard, Carlos Guerrero—but at least nobody except her father had witnessed it. This time had been worse—with her twin sisters announcing the news that their beloved sister Zoe had been sired by another man and was not a true Balfour after all.

Scenting blood—the paparazzi had been baying around the fabulous family mansion for days—and once again the Balfour name had been splashed all over the papers. Those words Kat had become so used to, whenever her family's name was mentioned, were once again the hot topic of the day. Words that still had the power to wound, no matter how many times she'd heard them.

Scandal.

Shame.

Secrets.

And the truth was that, yes, the Balfours were brimming with all of those things—and more. But just because they were rich, didn't mean they were impervious to pain or hurt. Prick them, and they bled—just like everybody else. Nobody saw *that*, of course, and nobody ever would—well, certainly not in Kat's case. She allowed herself a grim smile. Because the moment you showed hurt, you made yourself vulnerable—and vulnerability was the most dangerous thing of all. Didn't she know that better than anyone?

She stared out of the car window, reminding herself how she'd coped with the latest indignity. The same way that she always coped. She'd cut loose and run from the family estate. Not far, it was true—only as far as London—where she had booked into a hotel, using a fake name and a vast pair of sunglasses to hide behind. Until her father had rung her yesterday morning offering her an 'opportunity.'

Why had she felt a momentary wave of suspicion? Was it because that although Oscar was her true blood father, he had never been close to her heart in the same way as her beloved stepfather, Victor? Kat blinked back the tears which sprang to her eyes and replaced them with the defiant expression she had perfected. She wasn't going to think about her stepfather, or the past. She just *wasn't.* Because that way lay madness and regret and all those other painful emotions which she fought like crazy to keep at bay.

Nonetheless, her voice had been wary as she'd replied, 'What kind of opportunity, Daddy?'

There had been a pause. Had she imagined the unfamiliar steely quality which had entered his voice? 'The kind of opportunity which should be seized,' he said flatly. 'Didn't you tell me at the ball the other night that you were bored with your life, Kat?'

Had she said that? In a moment of weakness, had she been stupid enough to let on to the patriarch of the Balfour clan that a stream of loneliness as deep as a river seemed to be coursing through her veins?

'Did I?'

'Indeed you did. So why not grab at the opportunity for a change of scene and a change of air. How does a boat trip round the Mediterranean sound?'

It sounded exactly what she needed. Some good sea air and the chance to escape. And even though her father had tantalisingly refused to give her any more details, Kat knew it would be a treat. Because despite the impatience Oscar occasionally felt towards his daughters, deep down he loved nothing more than to lavish life's extravagances on them.

Which was why she was now reclining in the back of a luxury limousine, heading for the glamorous port of Antibes, while outside the brilliant Provençal sun beat down on all the wealthy holidaymakers. The glittering sea was shaded brilliant colours of cobalt and azure and the port was crammed with the biggest motor yachts you would find anywhere in the world. But that was the south of France for you—all glamour and glitz and buckets of money.

With a slickness perfected by years of practice, Kat pushed away her troubled thoughts as the limo slid to a halt next to a line of beautiful, bobbing yachts.

'There it is, miss,' said the driver, pointing to the biggest boat of all—where a couple of white-uniformed crew members were moving purposefully around the deck.

Suddenly, her mood was forgotten as Kat stared up at the most amazing-looking yacht she'd ever seen. With its long, aerodynamic shape and pointed prow, it rose up out of the water like some dazzling seabird. She could see a polished wooden deck and the turquoise glimmer of a swimming pool—as well as the ultimate convenience of a helicopter pad.

'Oh, wow,' she said, lips softening into a smile. Since babyhood, she had mixed in exalted and rich circles and knew that superyachts cost a fortune to own and maintain—but this magnificent vessel really was in a league of its own. It was…*spectacular.* Tourists were standing taking photographs of it and briefly Kat wondered who the owner could possibly be—and why her father had tantalisingly refused to tell her.

The name gave few clues. Painted in dark, curving letters along the side were the words *Corazón Frío.* Behind her dark glasses, Kat's eyes narrowed. Meaning *what*, precisely?

She was certainly no linguist—but even she could recognise that the language was Spanish. Her heart skipped an erratic beat. As was the only man who had ever slapped her down and humiliated her in public.

And who had haunted her dreams ever since.

A man with a hard, lean body and wild black hair and the coldest eyes she had ever seen.

Shaking away a memory even more unsettling than the uproar at last week's ball, Kat stepped out onto the quayside and couldn't help noticing that people had stopped to look at her.

But then, people always did. If you dazzled them with the externals, then they never really looked beyond to see the real person underneath. Clothes could be the armour that shielded you—that stopped people from getting too close. And it was better that way. Much better.

She was wearing a teeny pair of shorn-off denim shorts and a shrunken white T-shirt which gave the occasional glimpse of a flat midriff tanned the colour of pale caramel. Shiny black hair cascaded down over her shoulders and all the way down her back— and her Balfour blue eyes were hidden behind a pair of enormous shades. She knew exactly what kind of uniform to wear on this kind of rich and privileged yachting trip—and she had abided to it by the letter. You dressed down, but you wore as many status symbols as possible.

'Bring my bags, will you?' Kat said to the driver, before making her way towards the gangplank. Teetering a little on a pair of the season's most fashionable espadrilles, she saw a fair-haired man in uniform approaching her and she smiled.

'Hello. You're probably expecting me. I'm Kat Balfour,' she said.

'Yeah.' The man nodded, squinting his pale blue eyes at her, a small diamond glinting at his ear lobe. 'I thought you must be.'

Kat looked around. 'Any of the other guests here yet?'

'Nope.'

'And my…host?' How crazy it sounded not to even know him—or her—by name! Why hadn't she insisted her father tell her? *Because you were too busy trying to ingratiate yourself with him,* whispered the candidly cruel voice of her conscience. *Knowing that he was in an odd sort of mood and terrified that he might put a stop to your allowance—and then where would you be?* She could see the man looking at her quizzically and realised it would look faintly ridiculous if she had to ask him who his employer was! 'Has my host arrived yet?'

The man shook his head. 'Not yet.'

'Perhaps you'd like to take my luggage?' she suggested pointedly.

'Or you could do it yourself?'

Kat stared at him in disbelief. 'I beg your pardon?'

'I'm the engineer,' he said with a shrug. 'Not a baggage handler.'

Somehow she kept her smile fixed to her face. No point in getting into an argument with a deck-hand but she would certainly speak to his boss about his attitude. He would learn soon enough that *nobody* spoke to a Balfour like that. 'Then perhaps you could show me to my cabin,' she said coolly.

'My pleasure.' The man smiled. 'Follow me.'

Kat hadn't carried her own bags since she'd been expelled from her last school. These were heavy and they were cumbersome—and on the too-high shoes she was wearing, it wasn't the easiest task in the world to walk across the gleaming deck with any degree of grace.

If that was bad, then it suddenly began to get worse because just then they arrived at her cabin—and Kat looked around in disbelief. It had been ages since she'd stayed on a yacht, but in the past she had always been given the best and most prestigious accommodation available. Something near the deck, where you could climb out of bed and wander straight outside in the morning and be confronted by the ever-moving splendour of the sea. Or somewhere a little farther down towards the centre of the vessel—which meant that you were in the most stable part of the boat and buffeted from the possibility of too much movement.

But *this*.

Kat looked around. It was *tiny*. A cramped little bunk and barely any wardrobe space. No pictures on the walls and, even worse, *no porthole*! And someone had actually left a drab-looking piece of clothing hanging on the back of the door! She dropped her bags to the ground and turned to the man. 'Listen—'

'The name's Mike,' he interrupted. 'Mike Price.'

She wanted to tell him that his name was of no interest to her and that by the time the day was out he would be looking for a new job, but right then there were more pressing matters on her mind than the man's crass in-efficiency and overinflated sense of his own importance. Kat took in a deep breath. 'I think there's been some sort of mistake,' she said crisply.

'How come?'

'This cabin is much too small.'

'It's the one you've been assigned.' He shrugged his shoulders. 'Better take it up with the boss.'

Kat gritted her teeth. If only she knew who the boss was! But by now she knew she couldn't possibly lose face by asking this un-helpful man. 'I don't think you understand—'

'No, I don't think *you* understand,' inter-rupted the engineer brusquely. 'The boss likes his staff to put up and shut up—that's why he pays them so well.'

'But I'm not a member of staff,' she pro-tested. 'I'm a *guest* here.'

The man's eyes narrowed and then he laughed—as if she'd made some weird kind of joke. 'I don't think so. Or at least, that's not what I've been told.'

Kat felt the first tremor of apprehension. 'What are you talking about?'

Jerking his head in the direction of the garment which had caught her attention when she'd first walked in, Mike reached out and plucked it from the hook before handing it to her.

Kat looked at it blankly. 'What's this?'

'What's it look like?'

It took her a moment to realise—since it wasn't an item of clothing she was familiar with. 'An…an *apron*?' Momentarily, Kat's fingers tightened around the heavy fabric before she pushed it back at him, her heart beating wildly. 'What the hell is going on?'

Mike frowned. 'I think you'd better follow me.'

What could she do, other than what he suggested? Start unpacking all her expensive clothes and attempt to start storing them away in that rabbit's hutch of a room? Or maybe she should do what her gut instinct was telling her—which was to get off the wretched boat and forget about the whole idea of a holiday at sea.

She began to follow him through a maze of wood-lined corridors until at last he threw open a set of double doors and Kat quietly breathed a sigh of relief. Now *this* was more like it.

The room in which she now stood was the polar opposite of the poky cabin she'd just been shown. This had the enormous dimensions she was used to—a grand dining salon set out on almost palatial lines. Inlaid lights twinkled from the ceiling, but these were eclipsed by the blaze of natural light which flooded in through sliding French windows which opened up on to the deck itself.

There was a dining table which would have comfortably seated twelve people—though Kat noticed that only two places had been laid and used. Various open bottles were lined along the gleaming surface and candle wax had dripped all over a bone-china plate. At its centre was a beautiful blue-glass platter of exotic fruits and next to it sat a crystal goblet of flat champagne along with a carelessly abandoned chocolate wrapper.

Kat's lips pursed into a disapproving circle—wondering why on earth a member of staff hadn't bothered to clear it away. 'What a disgusting mess,' she observed quietly.

'Isn't it?' agreed Mike, laughing. 'The boss sure likes to party when he parties!'

So at least she now knew that the 'boss' was a man. And an untidy man, by the look of things. With a sudden smooth purring of powerful engines, the boat began to move—and Kat's eyes widened in surprise. But before she could register her inexplicable panic that they were setting sail so soon, something happened to wipe every thought clean from her mind.

The first was the sight of a bikini top—a flimsy little excuse for a garment in a shimmering gold material which was lying in a discarded heap on the polished oak floor. It was a blatant symbol of decadence and sex and, for a couple of seconds, the blood rushed hotly into her cheeks before she allowed herself to concentrate on the second.

Because the second was a photo of a man.

Kat's heart thundered as she stared at it—recognition hit her like a short sharp slap to the face.

The man in the photo must have been barely out of his teens, yet already his face was sombre and hardened by experience.

Black eyes stared defiantly straight into the lens of the camera, and his sensual lips curved an expression which was undeniably formidable.

He was wearing a lavishly embroidered glittering jacket, skintight trousers and some kind of dark and formal hat. It was an image which was unfamiliar and yet instantly recognisable—and it took a few moments for Kat to realise that this was the traditional garb of the bullfighter. But that realisation seemed barely relevant in the light of the horror which was slowly beginning to dawn on her.

That she was staring at a likeness of the young Carlos Guerrero.

Trying to conceal the shaking of her hands, she turned to Mike.

'Whose boat is this?' she croaked.

Mike's blond head was jerked in the direction of the photo, and he smiled. 'His.'

'C-Carlos?' Even saying his name sent shivers down her spine—just as the memory of his harsh words lancing through her still had the power to wound. 'Carlos Guerrero?'

'Sure. Who else?' Mike's expression grew even more curious. 'You didn't know?'

Of course she didn't know! If she had known, then she would never have set foot on the damned vessel—why, she wouldn't have gone within a million miles of it! But there was no way she was going to enlighten this smirking engineer about her misgivings, or the reason for them. She needed to assert her authority and get onto dry land again.

'I think there's been some kind of mix-up,' she said, her smooth tone belying the fast beating of her heart and sudden sense of urgency. 'And I'd like to go ashore. Please.'

'I'm afraid that won't be possible.'

Kat's eyes narrowed. 'What are you talking about?'

'Well, Carlos told me that a new domestic was arriving—and that her name was Kat Balfour.'

One word reverberated around the room and she repeated it, just in case she had misheard it. 'Domestic?' she repeated incredulously.

'Sure. You're Kat Balfour and there's six hungry crew on board.' He smiled. 'And we need someone to clean up after us and make our meals, don't we?'

It was so outrageous a statement to make

that for a moment Kat thought he must be having some kind of—extremely unfunny—joke at her expense. As if she was some kind of lowly deck-hand who was about to wait on a load of crew members! But one look at his face told her he was deadly serious. What the *hell* was going on?

'Get me off this wretched boat!' she said, as a sudden wave of panic washed over her. 'And I mean *immediately*!'

Again, he shrugged. 'Sorry, no can do. You'll have to take that up with the boss—I don't have the authority to clear it and we've left shore now. But I wouldn't advise you to try asking him any favours without clearing up this mess first. He'll be here later.'

Carlos Guerrero was coming *here*? Well, of course he was—if it was his boat. Kat blinked, feeling as if she had fallen into the middle of a raging sea, without any way of keeping herself afloat. And then another—equally shocking—thought occurred to her. Her father had arranged this trip for her. And if so—then *why*? Nothing seemed to make sense.

Yet none of that mattered—not now. She could take that up with him some other time.

The most important thing was to get away. To run. To escape before…

Before the man who had made her senses scream with longing put in an appearance.

Staring out of the windows to see that the port of Antibes was now just an array of glittering masts and boats in the distance, Kat realised she was trapped. Well and truly trapped—unless she could make this man Mike free her.

'Now listen to me, *Mike*,' she said, emphasising a cut-crystal accent which usually got her exactly what she wanted. 'Are you going to let me go, or not?'

'Sorry, love. No can do. More than my job's worth.'

'Right. Well, then, let me tell *you* something—and you'd better listen carefully. I am *not* your domestic and I am *not* going to cook or clean up for you and your fellow crew members. And what is more, I am certainly not going to clean up the mess left behind by your slob of a boss and his…his…*girl*friend. Do you understand?'

Mike shrugged. 'Loud and clear. Do what you like—I sure wouldn't want to be in your shoes when you tell Carlos that.' He glanced at his watch. 'I'd better get back to the captain. I'll leave you to calm down, and then you can come and find me and I'll show you the galley.'

And without another word, he turned and left, leaving Kat staring after him—shocked and stunned—her heart now racing with a fear which she hadn't felt in a long time. The one which she shoved deep down inside her, whenever it reared its dark and threatening head. That terrible tearing sensation of a hostile situation taking over and rendering her helpless….

Well, she wasn't helpless. And neither was she going to 'calm down' and acquaint herself with a galley she had no intention of ever using! Presumably she was stuck here until Carlos and the owner of the gold bikini top returned. A hot little curl of something which felt like *jealousy* began to unfurl inside her and Kat willed it to go away. She wasn't jealous of any poor unfortunate woman whose bikini top must have been removed by the arrogant Spaniard. Why, she…she *pitied* her—and what was more, she would have him arrested for kidnap when he finally *did* show his haughty face!

Pulling her cellphone from her bag, she desperately tried to get a connection—but for some reason, it refused to work. Even angrier now, and unable to bear the thought of just sitting there, Kat decided to explore the boat. And it didn't take her long to discover that her first impressions had been spot on. It wasn't just big, it was absolutely vast—and no expense had been spared during its outlay.

There was a cinema, a library and a well-stocked wine cellar—as well as an enormous sitting room which spread out onto the deck area. And she counted five luxury guest suites which even had their own elevator to connect them to the decks. This was wealth on a scale that far outweighed even her father's and briefly Kat found herself wondering how the Spaniard had made his money. Surely not through bullfighting?

By now she was feeling very hungry. It seemed a long time since her flight into France this morning and she never ate the disgusting food they served on scheduled flights. She needed to eat something, but was loath to go down into the galley in case she bumped into any of the other crew. Because wouldn't that seem like some silent admission of defeat?

Instead, she went back into the dining room and looked around to see what was left from the remains of the meal on the table. Not a lot. She ate a banana, two pomegranates and some rich, dark chocolate. And then, more out of defiance than desire, opened a bottle of wine whose label she recognised as being one of the world's finest and poured herself a large glassful.

Never a big drinker, the bouquet and depth of the claret was wasted on her, but at least the wine made her feel better. And more than a little rebellious. Her feelings of disbelief that this should actually be happening to her began increasingly to be replaced with a sense of fury. Just you *wait*, Carlos Guerrero, she vowed silently as she finished off the glass of costly wine and poured herself a second, before flopping down on a wide, squashy sofa which was heaped with cushions and staring out of the windows.

Watching the frilly white tips of the waves as the yacht powered its way over the sapphire sea, Kat was almost halfway through the bottle when she heard a sound which made her heart miss a beat. And then begin to accelerate with excitement.

It was the sound of a rich man's toy. The distinctive whirr-whirr chopping sound from overhead which could mean only one thing—a helicopter! And whoever was flying it would surely take pity on her and whisk her away from this luxurious prison.

Slamming the glass down on the table, Kat lurched to her feet. She would throw herself on the pilot's mercy. Inform him—or her—that she was being held here against her will and that she wished to be taken to the nearest police station.

But her rush to reach the deck and the helicopter pad seemed blighted—probably due to the amount of alcohol she'd drunk and her high-heeled espadrilles. To her horror, Kat slithered on the wooden floor and ended up sitting slam on her bottom. And by the time she had scrambled to her feet and got her bearings and worked out which of the many doors would give her access to the helicopter pad, she heard the heartbreaking sound of accelerating propellers. Which could only mean one thing. Please, please don't leave without me catching you, she prayed, even as she heard the loud rush of air which indicated that the craft was indeed now heading skywards.

With a small whimper she flung open one of the doors and hurled herself through it— only to be brought up short by a solid object as she cannoned into it.

A very solid object indeed.

'Buenas tardes, querida,' came a deeply accented voice which trickled over her senses like thick, dark honey.

And to her horror, Kat found herself staring up into the forbidding features of Carlos Guerrero.

CHAPTER TWO

KAT stared up into icy black eyes which were skating over her with undisguised disapproval. *'You!'* she accused, though her knees had turned to jelly and her heart was thundering so loudly that she felt quite faint. But what woman in the world wouldn't feel the same if confronted with that spectacular physique, clad in close-fitting black jeans and a soft white silk shirt—even if his handsome face was so cold that it might have been sculpted from some glittering piece of dark marble? 'Carlos Guerrero!' she breathed.

'Who were you expecting?' challenged Carlos silkily. 'It *is* my boat after all.'

Trying like mad to control the writhing tumult of her feelings, Kat glared at him. 'I thought…I thought I was in the middle of a nightmare, but it turns out it's true.'

'You mean you don't want to be here?' he mocked, his black eyes piercing into her like twin lasers.

Instinctively she stepped away. Away from the raw, masculine scent of him, and the heat which emanated from his powerful body. Away from the dangerous sizzle of sexuality which surrounded him like a dark and sensual aura and made her want to run her fingers through his riotous black curls.

'I'd rather be anywhere but here—with you,' she said. And yet didn't her words carry a hollow ring to them, because how could she protest at his presence when already she could sense his irresistible magnetism? The kind that made women—and her espe-cially—make complete fools of themselves. Well, not this time—that was for sure. *'Anywhere,'* she finished bitterly.

'I can assure you that the feeling is entirely mutual, *querida.*'

'Then let me go,' she breathed. 'Send for the helicopter and let it take me away.'

'No,' he negated harshly. 'I cannot and I will not.'

Kat looked at him in alarm. 'But you can't keep me here against my will!'

'Can't I?' A slow and mocking smile curved the edges of his lips. 'Aren't you even a little bit curious about why you're here— or did you think I was just longing for a little of your exclusive company?'

'Of course not,' she snapped. 'Any more than I'm longing for yours!'

'Good. Because, believe me—you were never going to be my number-one choice of sailing companion.'

Eyes narrowing, Carlos began to study her. She was beautiful, he conceded reluctantly. Even more beautiful than he remembered. Black hair tumbled like wild, dark silk over her shoulders, and her eyes were the most astonishing shade of blue he'd ever seen, framed by outrageously long, curling black lashes. Her lips were as pink as crushed rose petals—and her body was positively sinful.

Unfashionably curvy, she had the kind of legs which seemed to go on for ever—a fact emphasised by the tiny pair of denim shorts she wore, along with a pair of high-heeled espadrilles which showcased her painted toenails. Luscious-looking breasts were thrusting towards him as if crying out for him to cup them in the palms of his hands—their fullness set off perfectly by the simple white T-shirt which stretched tightly over them. So that they looked like two ripe peaches which had been smothered in cream…

But she left him cold. Completely cold. Her type always did. She was a predatory type of modern woman who flagrantly used her sexuality like a bitch in heat. Who saw what she wanted and then just went right out and took it. His mind took him back to the extravagant ball her family had thrown last year—when she had approached him with all the subtlety of a cheap *prostituta*, and his mouth hardened with remembered contempt.

¡Maldición! It was a pity he was forced to accommodate such a woman as this on the sanctuary of his beloved yacht—but he owed her father. Owed him more than he could ever say. And perhaps it would be amusing to snap this spoiled little madam from out of the privileged bubble in which she seemed to exist.

'Have you qu-quite finished?' questioned Kat in a voice which was shaking with rage and humiliation—for she had never been stared at like that before. She attracted attention, yes—but no man had ever had the temerity to study her as if she was being slowly stripped naked by a pair of contemptuous eyes. *And aren't you shaking for another reason?* questioned a taunting voice in her head. Aren't you shaking because you actually *like* him looking at you like that? Aren't your breasts tingling after his insolent scrutiny—and isn't there a kind of soft, aching pool where the denim is rubbing against the fork of your thighs?

'Finished?' echoed Carlos. 'Why, *querida*—I haven't even started.'

Kat's heart thumped, but she was damned if she would show even a trace of nerves. This man was nothing to her. *Nothing.* Fearlessly, she lifted her chin and iced him a look. 'Would you mind telling me what the hell is going on?'

Black eyes regarded her. 'You don't know anything?'

'Would I be asking if I did?' But then Kat remembered her father's strange reticence to disclose any details about her proposed boat trip, and now as she stared into the hard, cold face of the Spaniard her misgivings began to grow. 'This is something...something which has been cooked up between you and my father, isn't it?'

'Bravo,' he mocked softly, curious to see how she would react.

Kat's hands curled into two fists by the sides of her bare thighs. 'Well, I want to speak to him. Now!'

'Didn't anyone ever teach you to say *please*?'

'I don't really think that you're in a position to give me a lesson in manners when you're the one keeping me prisoner! I want some sort of explanation about why I've been...*kidnapped* by some wretched brute of a man like you!'

Carlos saw the icy blue fire of defiance spitting from her eyes and he felt a sudden rush of blood heating his veins. Oh, but he was going to enjoy taming her. To teach her that she could not just waltz through life, relying on her blindingly beautiful looks and her limitless bank account, taking exactly what she wanted, without a thought as to what the consequences might be.

'Just lose the hysteria—'

'But I—'

'I said *lose it,*' he snapped. 'And come with me.' He walked straight past her into the still-untidy cabin, his eyes narrowing with anger as he registered that she hadn't lifted a finger to clear anything away as he had expressly instructed she do. But he would deal with that. Later. Turning to face her, he pulled a cream envelope from the back pocket of his jeans and handed it to her. 'From your father,' he said.

Snatching the envelope from him, Kat was trembling as she ripped it open and withdrew a large sheet of paper, her eyes scanning over it quickly as she recognised her father's handwriting. *My dearest Kat,* it began.

It was the most bizarre document she had ever seen. Words flew off the page as if determined to grab her attention and she read them in rapidly mounting disbelief.

Words such as *powerful, proud and loyal—* and they were written in Latin too. *Validus, Superbus quod Fidelis.*

Kat's head was spinning as she read on.

*These are the words of our family motto,
which for many years used to guide the
Balfours. But something else used to guide
us too—a set of principles which were
known in the family as the rules.*

Kat's frown deepened. What on earth was
her father going on about? The letter continued.

*Of late, these principles have become
wilfully neglected and our name has become a laughing stock—both at home
and abroad. In many ways, I blame myself. The example I have set to my children over the years has been a poor one,
but I am determined that my daughters
will not replicate my chequered lifestyle.*

Then came the paragraph which made
Kat's blood run cold.

*Which is why I am cutting off your al-
lowance, Kat, and forcing you to earn
your keep for the first time in your life.
It will also ensure that you embrace the
concept of the word* commitment—

which is rule 6: run away from your problems once and you will run for ever.

You have spent your whole life running from your problems, Kat, but it is time that you learned to look them in the face. By facing problems, you defeat them. Running away is what cowards do, not Balfours. You need to figure out a direction for your life, instead of just drifting aimlessly. A little hard work might help focus your mind.

This is why I have arranged for you to work your passage on the yacht of Carlos Guerrero. He is a man I know and trust to set you on the right path. He is the only man I have ever seen stand up to you, and you cannot run away while you are at sea! Forgive me for what must seem like an extreme measure, my dearest Kat, but I am confident that one day you will be grateful that I took it.

Your loving father, Oscar

Kat's manicured nails dug into the expensive cream velour paper and it took a moment or two for her to compose herself enough to risk looking Carlos in the face. And when she did, it only increased her ire, for his black eyes were glittering with what looked like *pleasure*, and a smile of satisfaction was curving his lips.

'You knew about this!' she accused.

'Of course I did.'

'Rules? *Rules*,' she spluttered. 'It's outrageous.'

'I quite agree,' he said unexpectedly, and then his accented voice grew harsh. 'Completely outrageous that a woman of twenty-two has never done an honest day's work in her life!'

Kat swallowed. 'That's none of your business!'

'Oh, but it is, *querida*. Your father has made it my business by electing me as the poor unfortunate who has been forced to employ you—because I doubt that anyone else would!'

'I can't *believe* that Daddy would willingly subject me to…'

The black eyes challenged her. 'To *what*, *exactamente*?'

'To be holed up with a man who's world famous for his womanising!'

For a moment, Carlos didn't respond. The slur was an oft-repeated one which infuriated the hell out of him, and it was made by the press and the public at large simply because women had a terrible tendency to fall in love with him. And then to talk about it to whoever would listen—the way women always loved to talk when their hearts were smitten. But if he could have a euro for every woman he was supposed to have slept with, then his already-generous bank accounts would be overflowing.

He stared at the stunning brunette—almost marvelling at her gall and wondering how she, of all people, had the nerve to level such an accusation at him.

'But I'm extremely picky where women are concerned—you of all people should know that,' he drawled. 'After all, I turned *you* down, didn't I, *querida*? Even though you were pretty much begging me to make love to you.'

Kat flushed. Of all the most hateful... *hateful* things he could have said.

But it was true, wasn't it? That was the painful reality of it. She *had* thrown herself at him. Behaved in a way which had been completely foreign to her. Because despite her worldly appearance and air of sophistication, Kat was a disaster where men were concerned.

Sometimes her sisters teased her about her lack of boyfriends and Kat had often wondered if she would ever experience the kind of overwhelming emotional and sexual desire which other women spoke of. And yet she wasn't even sure she wanted to—because getting close to people meant that you could get hurt.

So she hid behind her outrageous outfits, presenting a fashionable, brittle exterior to the world—terrified that somebody would find her out and see through to the gaping insecurities inside. And it had always been easy, because she had never really felt stirred by a man. Not until last year's ball….

The dress she had worn had been pretty daring—even by her standards. Carefully constructed in scarlet satin, the low-cut bodice had left her breasts half bare and the thigh-high slashes of the skirt showed off her long legs as she walked. Precious gems had sparkled in her hair—with the famous Balfour Brilliant winking in a provocative diamond teardrop between her breasts.

Kat remembered descending the stairs into the grand ballroom, aware that all eyes had turned to watch her, but she had felt oblivious to their interest…as if she was half asleep, like a person in a dream.

And then she had seen him. Standing out among the hundreds of other guests like a bright planet in a clear night sky. Her heart had begun to thunder powerfully with some kind of ancient recognition and in that single moment she had understood what all the fuss was about. Why women fell in love at first sight. And why it could happen without reason, or warning.

Carlos Guerrero.

He had been wearing a formal suit—the stark black clothes exquisitely tailored to emphasise every hard sinew of his impressive physique and his long, lean legs and narrow hips. His black hair had been longer than the other men's in the ballroom—and wilder too. Yes, that was the best way to describe what Carlos Guerrero had looked like that night—

there was a sense that beneath the immaculate exterior, he was untamed. Proud, dangerous and sexy—he seemed more alive than anyone else she'd ever set eyes on, and just looking at him sparked a longing as old as time.

The only problem was that he was with a woman—a serene-looking woman who barely wore a scrap of make-up—but then, she didn't really need to. Not when you were as naturally beautiful as that. Kat remembered her dismay as she'd stared at his partner's soft, even features and the elegant chignon of her hair. Her gown was a fluid fall of cream, quietly emphasising a stunning figure, and two luminous pearl studs gleaming at her ears were her only adornment.

Kat had suddenly felt like an overdressed Christmas tree in comparison—yet that didn't stop her wanting the man with a hunger which made her feel positively weak.

But he had refused to play ball—his black eyes had been cold, his manner dismissive, when she was introduced to him. Carlos Guerrero was his name, and she remembered thinking that it was the most gorgeous name in the world.

Kat did everything to get him to notice her—but because she'd never had to try with a man before, she tried too hard. Much too hard. Every time she thought he was watching her, she had played up to it like mad. Tipping her head back and giggling. Letting her eyes close in dreamy surrender. Yet she might as well have been trying to get a reaction from a stone for all the good it did. Until at last, when his lovely partner had disappeared in the direction of the cloakrooms, Kat had spotted him going out onto the terrace. And shamelessly she had followed him.

The moon had been full, the night thick with the scent of jasmine and honeysuckle, and there was an air of promise bubbling within her—a sense that, in that moment, anything was possible if only she had the courage to reach out and take it. Overladen with unfamiliar longing, Kat had walked towards him.

'Hello,' she said softly.

His black eyes had narrowed and he had nodded his head in a kind of resigned recognition. 'You're the woman who's been flirting with me so outrageously all evening,' he said slowly.

'H-have I?' Thankfully, the darkness had hidden her sudden rise in colour. But hadn't her sisters told her that it was an equal world now and that women could approach men these days, if they really wanted to? 'I wondered, would you…would you like to dance?' she had asked, her careless tone disguising the fierce pounding of her heart but she could feel the tightening of her breasts as she moved a little closer.

She would remember the look on his face for as long as she lived. Something which looked uncomfortably like anger and which quickly grew into cold contempt as he briefly stared down at the large diamond which glittered between the scrap of scarlet satin straining over her bust.

'Do you always behave like such a tramp, *querida*?' he bit out with soft derision. 'So that you flaunt your wares like a trader in the marketplace? Or do you only want a man when he is with someone else?'

Cringing beneath the icy disdain in the Spaniard's eyes, Kat barely noticed the figure who had now appeared in the doorway and who stood watching them.

'B-but—'

Putting his mouth to her ear so that only she could hear, she would never forget his contemptuous words.

'You are dressed like a hooker and you are behaving like a hooker!' he had hissed. 'So why don't you go and cover yourself up, and then take the time to learn a few lessons on the correct way to conduct yourself in public.'

After this blistering attack, he had sauntered back into the ballroom—past her father, who had silently been observing them—and returned to the beautiful woman in cream. Where, according to her sisters, he had tenderly wrapped her in a soft shawl and had taken her off into the night—leaving Kat alone with her shame and her disbelief that she could have behaved in such a way. That she could have been so *predatory*.

Her sisters had also taken great delight in informing her that not only was the man a famous ex-bullfighter, but that he could have his pick of the most gorgeous women in the world. Which had only made her feel worse.

And that had been the last time she'd seen Carlos Guerrero.

Until now.

Painful memories cleared and Kat realised that the Spaniard was watching her and that she was still holding the letter from her father which had put her in this man's power.

So forget the terrible way you behaved and the cruel way he rebuffed you. That's all in the past now. Why not appeal to his sense of logic instead? Forcing a smile, she turned to him. 'Look, Carlos, you can't want this any more than I do,' she urged.

Carlos considered her words. When her father had asked him to employ her, his first instinct had been to bat the suggestion away. Because he wasn't into playing mentor. Particularly not to spoiled little rich girls who lived their lives like greedy children let loose in a candy store.

So why the hell *hadn't* he refused this challenge?

Because Oscar Balfour had been good to him, had helped him set up the property business which had made him a very wealthy man indeed. For there had been a time when nobody wanted to know the angry young Spaniard battling to make a new life for himself. When Carlos had been nothing but an ex-matador who had spent every penny he'd earned, Oscar had taken a risk by giving him a sizeable loan. Had trusted him at a time when few others had—and a man never forgot something like that.

No, he could not have turned down Oscar's request—no matter how unwanted the suggestion had been.

'Since you ask—no, I don't want this at all. I have much better things to do with my time than playing nursemaid to a spoiled brat,' he said coolly. 'But my wishes are irrelevant. Your father asked for my help, and so I'm giving it. I owe him.' He shrugged. 'And it wasn't exactly onerous to employ you on my boat. I'm always looking for an extra pair of hands.'

Kat shook her head. 'You want money?' she questioned desperately. 'I can write you a cheque if you set me free.'

For a moment Carlos shook his head, appalled by the sheer impudence of her offer. Did she think that he could be bought, or that money could buy her out of any tight corner? He guessed she did—for hadn't it been lavished on her during all her life? Suddenly, he found himself remembering the unalloyed poverty of his early years. Of the way his mother had spent every waking hour cleaning for the rich—her careworn hands red and cracked, her eyes dark from lack of sleep. And Carlos felt another wave of contempt for this girl who had always had things so easy.

'You forget that buying your way out is no longer an option since your father has cut off your allowance,' he drawled.

'But I have money I can access!' she declared. 'Jewels I can sell!'

'Just not when you're in the middle of the Mediterranean, hmm?' he countered sarcastically.

And suddenly the reality of the situation hit her. Him. And her—stuck in a boat whose dimensions seemed to be diminishing by the second. 'I'm...I'm sure we can come to *some* sort of agreement,' she said wildly.

'I don't think so.' The black eyes narrowed and he glanced over to the tight, white T-shirt and the tops of her bare brown thighs which were so graphically showcased in the tiny pair of shorts. 'Unless you're offering payment in kind, of course?' he added insultingly, his voice soft. 'You're certainly dressed as if you are.'

It took Kat a moment for his words to register, and when she realised exactly what he meant she felt a strange, burning fury— and a renewed sense of rebellion.

How could she bear to be trapped on board with such a powerfully attractive man as this—especially when he had made his contempt for her so apparent? Expected to cook and clear up after him like a servant! Heart now pounding with anticipation of what she was about to do, Kat gave him one final glare of defiance.

'Maybe you're used to paying for sex!' she retorted, and had the brief satisfaction of seeing his lips tighten in anger. 'And maybe you're used to calling all the shots. But not this time. I won't be kept prisoner here by you, Señor Guerrero!'

Without warning, she ran across the salon and out onto the deck, tearing off her espadrilles before scrambling up the side of the guard-rail. At least it was as wide as a small ledge. Wide enough to dive from.

For a few seconds, Kat experienced a

moment of wild exhilaration as she stared down into the dark sapphire of the sea, before taking a deep, deep breath. And then, with the sound of Carlos Guerrero's furious shouts ringing in her ears, she plunged into the blue water beneath.

CHAPTER THREE

THE shock of impact and the cold temporarily winded her, but Kat was a good swimmer—when she'd lived in Sri Lanka, she'd spent so much time in the water that they used to call her Little Fish. But the trouble was that swimming in pools or striking out from a beach was quite different to swimming in deep sea like this, and it took only minutes for the enormity of what she'd done to sink in. Her limbs felt heavy and weighted—the denim shorts seeming to weigh a ton—and it occurred to her that she had drunk two glasses of wine and that her judgement may have been blunted. But still she kept striking out—and it seemed more as if she was lashing out against life, and fate. Hot tears of fury mingled with the salt of the sea on her face, until she realised that she was in danger of getting completely exhausted, and so she began to tread water.

Turning on her back, she could see that the *Corazón Frío* had stopped, and that a little boat had been lowered and was heading her way—but before it could reach her, something else did. Or rather, someone. A streamlined body which was powering its way through the water towards her and which suddenly emerged from the depths like some golden-wet colossus.

Sleek black hair plastered to his skull, Carlos reached out and caught hold of her, his face contorted with fury. But the relief he felt at having located her was overwhelming and it washed over him in a great wave. *The little fool. The stupid little fool.*

'Let me—' uselessly, Kat wriggled against the formidable strength of his body '—go!'

His mouth was close to her wet ear as he trod water, her breasts flattened against his chest as his hands tightened around her waist and held her closer. 'You are not going *anywhere, querida,*' he gasped. 'You will stay right here until the tender reaches us—or you'll have us both damned well drowned!'

The awful thing was that for the first time in her life Kat felt safe. Truly and properly safe. His arms were so strong and powerful and his hold on her so firm that she felt as if nothing or no one could hurt her just as long as this man was holding her. And how crazy was that—in view of the circumstances? If she could place her trust and her confidence in a man who clearly despised her, then surely that really *did* mean her judgement was terminally flawed.

'Damn you,' she whispered shakily.

'No, damn *you*,' he shot back furiously. 'I was warned that you liked running away—but nobody told me you'd be a liability!'

The boat reached them, with Mike at the helm, and Kat was helped aboard—acutely aware that the flat of Carlos's palm was shoving firmly on one sodden denim-covered buttock from behind. Then he levered himself up and into the boat and helped to sit her down. His feet were bare, the black jeans were soaking and the white silk shirt now clung to his chest like a second skin—the fabric so fine that she could see the whorls of black hair through it. Suddenly, Kat felt quite weak as he crouched down beside her, placing one hand at the small of her back to help support her.

A pair of stony black eyes were levelled at her. 'Don't ever try pulling a stunt like that again,' he warned softly. 'Understand?'

Kat was aware that Mike had his back to them as he steered the little boat towards the yacht. Was he diplomatically pretending not to listen, or would it even make any difference if he was? If she started screaming hysterically like one of those women in an old black-and-white movie, was it likely that Mike would turn round to the 'boss' he clearly revered and demand that he return her to shore immediately? No, it was not.

Which meant she was stuck here. Stuck with the only man she'd ever felt a physical connection towards—and still did, if she was honest. Even when she was physically and mentally exhausted.

'Understand?' repeated Carlos.

Staring into eyes which were as emotionless as rock itself, Kat swallowed down the salt taste of the sea. 'Do I have any choice?' she questioned bitterly.

'No, *querida*, you do not—other than to work your way on this voyage and prove that you can do it. To stand on your own two feet for once…if you think you can.' Black eyes challenged her. 'After that, you can walk away and we need never set eyes on each other again.'

The aftermath of all the emotion suddenly hit her like a roller coaster, along with a dull aching which had now begun to gather at the front of her forehead, and Kat began to shiver uncontrollably.

Carlos frowned, but the arm which was still at her slender back tightened by a fraction. Her face was white—almost translucent—and her lips were turning a faintly blue colour. *Y por Dios*—but she suddenly looked fragile. Like a little doll who might snap in two.

'Hurry up!' he snapped at Mike as the small craft moved alongside the larger vessel. 'She's freezing!'

Kat was vaguely aware of being lifted onto the deck of the *Corazón Frío* and aware too that Carlos had curtly dismissed Mike and the rest of the crew who had appeared to help.

And then, to her astonishment, he picked her up as if he picked up full-grown women every day of the week, and carried her along one of the wood-lined corridors to some sort of cabin. But it wasn't the same poky little cabin which Mike had taken her to earlier.

Dazed by shock and the sensation of being held within his strong arms, she looked around at the unfamiliar luxurious surroundings. 'Th-this isn't m-my c-cabin,' she protested, her teeth chattering uncontrollably as he set her down. Her eyes widened as her heart began an erratic pounding. 'It's n-not *yours*, is it?'

'Mine?' Carlos gave a forbidding smile as he set her back down on her feet. 'Please don't overestimate your appeal, *querida*. I don't take idle little rich girls to my bed.'

His cruel words should have hurt but Kat was now feeling so numb that she could barely move, let alone protest at his rudeness. Disconcertingly, he had started tugging at her top and she could feel the sudden heat of his hand against her frozen skin.

'W-what do you think you're doing?' she breathed.

'What the hell does it look like?' he demanded, but his voice sounded distorted and he hated the sudden urgent escalation of his heart. Damn her, he thought—and damn her sleek and inviting body! 'I'm getting you out of these wet clothes before I have to cable ashore for a doctor.'

Kat expelled a shallow breath because even through her icy confusion she liked the feel of his skin against her skin. She liked it a lot. She felt faint as he peeled off the sodden T-shirt and saw his body tense as he tossed it aside, a look of grim determination etched on his face. Next, he began undoing her bra with lightning-fast dexterity, until that was also cast unceremoniously to the floor. Then, pushing her down on the bed with a touch which was more gentle than she would ever have expected, he tossed a blanket over her. A blanket so warm and so soft that it felt as if she had been enveloped in a cloud. Teeth still chattering, Kat clutched at it with convulsive fingers.

'That's b-bliss,' she stumbled, her eyelids feeling weighted as the temptation to sleep began to steal over her.

'Take off those damned shorts,' he demanded on a snarl, but either she wasn't listening or she hadn't heard him. Or maybe she was in shock. He remembered the scent of wine on her breath and his mouth hardened. Or drunk.

Carlos had been the greatest bullfighter of his generation and the adroitness of his wrist action had caused ecstatic crowds to sigh in admiration. Yet such skilfulness had bizarrely deserted him when it came to removing a tiny pair of soaking denim shorts from the delectable bottom of Miss Kat Balfour. His only saving grace was that she seemed scarcely aware of the exquisite torture she was unknowingly inflicting upon him.

Only when a tiny thong had been tugged down over her goose-bumpy thighs, and she was completely naked beneath the blanket, did he step away—and then very gingerly, for he was more aroused than he had been in a long time. *¡Maldición!*

Picking up another of the cashmere throws, he floated that down over her for good measure and heard her sigh before she snuggled down into its soft folds. Her eyelids had fluttered to a close and rested on her pale cheeks in two dark feathery arcs. Her lips—now restored to a rose-petal hue—were parted and she gave a soft sigh and snuggled into the pillow while he watched her. With her damp hair fanned over the pillow, she looked pure—almost innocent.

But appearances could be deceptive, he reminded himself acidly, forcing himself to remember all the reasons why he disliked her. Predatory, unscrupulous and spoiled—she was antithesis of all the qualities he admired in a woman. Carlos admired hard work and humility far more than privilege, or position.

He had appeared at her family ball with a woman on his arm, but Kat Balfour hadn't cared about that, had she? No. She hadn't cared about a thing except homing in on him like a sex-seeking missile. Why, even when she was half drowned she was somehow managing to send out the instinctive message of the siren.

And just for a moment back then, he had responded, hadn't he? Responded big time.

Carlos's mouth hardened with fury at his own susceptibility. He should have demanded that her father pay him danger money to have taken on this task. Better still, he should have told Oscar Balfour to find someone else. But it was too late to back out now. And surely this snip of an Englishwoman—no matter how flighty or petulant—could never be compared to the challenges he had faced in the bullring?

Her arm had moved back to lie above her head and he stared down at the diamond-encrusted wristwatch which dangled from her fragile wrist—an expensive-looking piece which looked as if it was completely wrecked by sea water. He saw the outline of her luscious curves beneath the fine cashmere and knew he did not dare risk removing the watch. Not unless he planned to wake her up in a way which he could—suddenly and inexplicably—imagine all too vividly....

His throat thickening, Carlos walked over to the door and snapped out the light, knowing that he had to get the hell out of there.

CHAPTER FOUR

KAT awoke to an unfamiliar room and an unfamiliar feeling.

Eyelids fluttering open, she gazed around in confusion as she registered the strange rocking sensation, trying to work out where she was and how she'd got here. The room was luxurious, lined with gleaming wood and Venetian mirrors. Persian rugs lay strewn on the floor and she could see her two bags standing next to the wardrobe. And hanging on the back of the door was that damned apron. She was on Carlos Guerrero's luxury yacht!

Groaning, she propped herself up on the bank of soft pillows. She was lying on top of a huge bed, covered by two enormous cashmere throws. And… Kat froze as the palms of her hands skated down over her body as if to verify her initial fears. Because beneath the blankets she was *completely naked*.

That would explain the unfamiliar feeling. She always slept covered up. Always. Cosy, warm pyjamas in winter and a lightweight cotton-lawn version during the warmer weather. It dated back to childhood—a habit she'd never quite got out of, a habit more deeply engrained by never quite knowing what the night might throw at you....

With a start, she sat up, her eyes automatically straying to her wristwatch and blinking in confusion to see that it was shiny with droplets of water—and that it had stopped completely.

Haphazardly events came flooding back in a disconcerting stream. Being tricked onto the yacht and told that she was to be some sort of servant to Carlos Guerrero. And then... Kat bit her lip as she remembered trying to flee. Diving overboard into the Mediterranean and Carlos coming after her and bringing her back. *Had she really done something that crazy?*

Hanging over the back of the chair were her little denim shorts, T-shirt, her bra and tiny thong—and with a heated rush of blood to her cheeks, Kat recalled Carlos peeling the garments from her body. *And the way that had made her feel.*

Locking the door and picking up one of her bags, she stumbled into the bathroom, shocked at the sight of her white face and the mess of black hair. But a hot shower and an intense toothbrushing session soon had her feeling almost normal as she riffled through her bags for something to wear. But what? The clothes she'd brought had been chosen for the purpose of not doing very much at all—other than lazing around on deck and relaxing in the sun.

Yet since she had been duped into coming here, why should she care that many of the outfits at her disposal were completely inappropriate for her lowly new post? Especially when there was *no way* she was going to take that post on—no matter what her father said!

Defiantly, Kat pulled a slithery silk slip-dress over her head. It was made by that season's hottest new designer and it had sold out weeks before it had even hit the shelves. Only the favoured few had managed to get their hands on it—and Kat had been among them. Falling to mid-thigh, it showed off the even caramel tan of her legs and was an extremely flattering fit—so why *shouldn't* she wear it?

But her heart was pounding with something which felt like trepidation, as she went off to find Carlos Guerrero.

Guided by the strong aroma of coffee which was drifting in from the direction of one of the decks, she stepped out into brilliant light, blinking a little and wondering if she should go back for a hat. Sunlight was dancing in a frenzied light show on the sapphire sea, and the sky was a piercingly clear shade of azure. At any other time and in any other place, Kat might have sighed and simply appreciated the scenic splendour—but now her attention was elsewhere. Diverted to the infinitely more human splendour which was lying just a few short feet away….

Carlos was sprawled on some sort of huge chaise longue—tapping away at some sleek-looking computer, wearing a pair of low-slung white jeans, an open white shirt and a pair of dark shades. Nearby, was a large table on which stood a steaming coffee pot and a basket of different breads. But despite the sudden gnawing hunger at her stomach, Kat paid the food no attention.

For a moment she simply stood there and observed the man whose blue-black hair glinted in the sunlight. Powerful and lean, his body looked indolent and relaxed—the way you sometimes saw those black pumas in wildlife programmes looking when they'd just been fed. Kat's stomach flipped as she registered the broad shoulders, the narrow jut of his hips and the long legs which seemed to go on for ever. And yet coupled with her undeniable attraction towards him was a faint sense of wariness and the reluctant acknowledgement that this was the kind of man whose will could never be bent to the wishes of a woman...

Carlos glanced up as Kat walked out on deck towards him and felt his body tense. He wondered if she realised that the powerful sun was angling on her tiny sundress and outlining her body in eye-popping detail, making it appear as if she wasn't wearing anything at all.

Of course she realised, he told himself cynically. Women like her used their clothes to showcase their sexuality. A sexuality which she seemed to have no qualms about putting out at every opportunity and which he was just going to have to ignore. His mouth hardened as he averted his eyes from her magnificent breasts.

'So you have decided to grace us with your presence at last,' he observed coolly.

And stupidly, despite his disparaging tone, Kat's heart began beating furiously. 'Wh-what time is it?'

'Eleven.'

'In the morning?'

He glanced around at the gold-dappled splendour of the deck. 'We don't usually have sunshine at eleven in the evening,' he answered sardonically. 'Even in the Mediterranean.'

'Eleven!' she exclaimed, ignoring his sarcasm. 'You mean I've slept for…for…'

'Hours,' he agreed tightly. 'Too much burning the candle at both ends, no doubt. Either that or the wine you drank made you sleep.' He lifted the dark shades away from his eyes and stared directly into her face, fixing her with a glittering black gaze. 'And I see that you opened the Pétrus.'

Kat remembered the anger she had felt at being trapped and told she was to work on the Spaniard's yacht. Remembered too the discarded gold bikini top—and once again a stab of something which felt uncomfortably like jealousy unsettled her. So what if she *had* drunk half a bottle of his very expensive wine? 'Sorry. I just couldn't resist it,' she said guilelessly. 'Was it very expensive?'

There was a pause. 'Very.'

'Oh.' She opened her eyes very wide. Maybe if she annoyed him enough he might drive her to the nearest shore himself. 'And did you mind?'

Mind? What he minded more than anything was her careless attitude and the way those bright blue eyes sparked at him so defiantly. She *wanted* him to mind, he realised, and would have liked to have shown his displeasure in a very primitive way indeed. By upending her on his lap and slapping the palm of his hand against her delectable bottom. 'You have very good taste in wine, *querida*,' he observed.

Kat stared at him suspiciously. This was not the reaction she was expecting. 'I…I have?'

'*Sí. Absolutamente.* There will, of course, have to be some adjustment to your wages as a consequence.' He shrugged as he saw her perfect lips part in a disbelieving circle. 'Though naturally, it will simply be a token gesture, since no galley-hand could ever afford to pay the full price for such a bottle of wine.'

Suspicion turned to frustration. 'You're not still maintaining this fiction about me working on your boat, are you?' she demanded.

Carlos pushed his laptop into a shady corner beneath the lounger and rose effortlessly to his feet. 'I can assure you that it is not a fiction, Kat. It is a done deal and I have given my word to your father that I will employ you—despite the fact that you do not seem to have a single useful qualification to your name.'

'That's none of your business—'

'I'm afraid it is. I have agreed to take you on—and one of the first things you'd better learn is that as a member of my crew you will be expected to be punctual at all times.'

'But I'm not—'

'I am not interested in your objections.' Once again, his clipped words sliced through her stumbled responses. 'All I know is that you've made an appalling start.' His gaze flicked over the mutinous tremble of her lips and he felt an undeniable beat of pleasure. 'However, in view of the *exceptional* circumstances, I'll let you off this time—just don't try it again. In future I want you on deck by seven. The crew can fix themselves breakfast, but I expect you to attend to what I like. Good coffee, a little fruit and some bread. My needs are very simple.' His eyes mocked her. 'You'll make a light lunch for everyone and a rather more elaborate meal for the evening. And you'll be expected to keep the decks and cabins clean, though obviously not the crew's. Understand?'

There was a moment of disbelieving silence while Kat looked at him with shock and dislike as he shot out his list of outrageous demands. 'No, I don't think *you* understand,' she answered furiously. 'You've had your little *joke*, Carlos, but it's gone on for long enough. I don't want to stay here and I don't want to work for you. I...I want to go back to shore.' There was a pause while he looked at her expectantly and she forced herself to say it, even though the word felt as if it might choke her. 'Please.'

Carlos clapped his hands in mock applause. '¡*Bravo!*' he said silkily. 'We make progress! The spoiled Englishwoman—she learns what it is to be polite!'

Kat looked at him hopefully. 'So you'll take me?'

'I cannot,' he snapped. 'Surely your attention span isn't so short that you've already forgotten the letter from your father which you read last night?'

She thought back to that ridiculous set of rules her father had set out—the one Carlos had presented her with when he'd arrived on board. 'Of course I haven't forgotten, but my father has clearly taken leave of his senses!'

'Wrong again.' Carlos's lips flattened into an uncompromising line. 'In fact, I think his intervention is long overdue and it's time you stopped acting like a spoilt little princess. One who snaps her fingers and thinks the world owes her a living. An overindulged rich girl who sees just what she wants and then takes it. I cannot believe that nobody has ever accused you of it before. *Princesa.*'

Kat stood as he taunted her with the word, but now her heart had begun to thunder erratically as ice-cold tentacles of fear began to tiptoe down her spine, in spite of the warmth of the morning sun. Fear that she usually kept battened down, hidden away like a dark secret. Didn't he realise that she, of all people, couldn't cope with the idea of being trapped? That she had witnessed enough violence and horror to last a lifetime—and that sometimes she needed to run from those memories. Quite literally, to run.

Like a dark and acrid poison, reminders of that time rose up in her mind, but she blocked them. The way she'd been blocking them ever since her world had been turned upside down by the death of her stepfather and nothing had ever been the same again. She never talked about it with anyone. *Anyone.* Not all the counsellors or psychologists they'd paid for over the years. Not her mother or her father. *Nobody.* And she certainly wasn't going to start with this arrogant beast of a man who seemed to bring out the very worst in her.

'I am not going to stay here slaving away

for an arrogant man who insults me,' she blurted out. 'And what is more, you can't force me to!'

'Oh, but I can. And I will,' he returned implacably as he rose from the table. 'One day you may even thank me for it.'

'The hell I will!'

He gave a short laugh. 'Oh, but I can see that you are in urgent need of subduing, *Princesa.* And if you're planning any more theatrical displays like diving in and swimming to shore, then forget it. I might not be so inclined to jump in and save you next time.'

He saw her bright blue gaze moving distractedly round the deck, as if searching there for some other kind of getaway. 'What's more, if you're thinking you might spirit yourself away on one of my motorboats, I'd better warn you that I'll be keeping all the ignition keys close to me. And the rest of the crew have instructions not to take you ashore, no matter how beguilingly you decide to ask them.' His black eyes glittered a stark warning. 'So don't bother wasting your time trying to escape.'

Kat stared at him. If being trapped with him wasn't bad enough, his cavalier and *patronising* attitude made it a hundred times worse.

And suddenly, all her feelings of hurt and rage and frustration welled up into an urgent need to make him realise that she meant what she said.

'Let me off this boat at once, you…you… overbearing…*beast*!' she half sobbed, launching herself towards him before she stopped to think about the wisdom of her actions, drumming her fists furiously against the rock-solid wall of his chest. *'Just let me go!'*

For a moment, Carlos didn't react to the warm intoxication of her proximity and the realisation that the soft curve of her hips was only a thrust away. He was known for his restraint, for a steely self-control which had seen him turn down more women than most men would dream of.

And yet now he could feel the first stealthy silken tug of sexual awakening as the coldly analytical side of his brain fought against the escalating clamour of his senses.

His mouth hardened. He didn't even *like* Kat Balfour. So why was his body hardening with unbearable tension, its demands beginning to wash over him in hot, sweet waves?

'Let me *go*!' she repeated, as the drumming of her fists increased.

'No,' he grated, staring down into her bright blue eyes with dislike. 'What a little hypocrite you are, Kat. Women who want men to let them go don't start pressing themselves against them and flaunting their bodies in such a way that shows they're just begging to be kissed. Do they?'

She opened her mouth to deny it but as she stared up into his face she could see that his eyes were no longer like stone. In fact, they blazed like ebony fire as they raked over her. And despite the condemnation in his tone, Kat's words died on her lips as, with a growl of desire and fury, Carlos lowered his head towards hers and began to kiss her.

She swayed as she felt the hard pressure of his mouth driving down on hers, clutching at the silken-clad expanse of his shoulders, her thoughts swirling as their flesh met and melded. This was *bliss*, she thought distractedly, as she clung to him, heart beginning to pound as she felt the first flick of his tongue.

Wasn't this how a kiss was *supposed* to feel? What she'd been holding out for all her life? *'Oh,'* she moaned helplessly, as the pressure of his lips increased. 'Oh!'

¡Dios!

Carlos felt her instant capitulation, as sweet and responsive as he had guessed she might be. As he deepened the kiss, he could feel her breasts peaking against him. Sweet, neat breasts—like tender peaches just waiting to be bitten into. He wanted to take one into his hand, to rub his thumb against its ripe nub. And then to delve his fingers beneath the soft silk of her sinful little dress, to discover if she was wearing proper panties this time. Or another of those X-rated G-strings…

For several agonisingly tempting moments, he imagined plunging into her, imagined her hungry little cries as she urged him on. And then, just as suddenly as the kiss had started, he tore his lips away from hers, stepping back as if she was contaminated, his furious gaze raking over her flushed cheeks and darkened eyes.

Frustrated desire found an outlet in heated accusation as he willed the frantic thudding of his heart to lessen and the fierce aching at his groin to stop throbbing and tormenting him. 'Do you always act like this—like a sex-starved tramp?' he demanded unevenly. 'Are you one of these women who are ruled by the hunger of their bodies, perhaps—who grab at the nearest man whenever he happens to be available?'

The harsh words hurt, but presumably that had been his intention. 'C-can't the same be said about you?' she shot back, stung, because he was so wrong in his character assessment of her that it would have been almost laughable had it not been quite so insulting. Clamping her arms around her still-tender breasts she hid her arousal and confusion behind a shield of sarcasm. 'I mean, obviously you have a fantastic technique—'

'That was never in any doubt, *Princesa.*'

'I'm just appalled at my own reaction to an uncaring brute like you,' she choked. 'Especially since you had another woman in your arms only yesterday!'

Carlos found his gaze drawn irresistibly to the rapid rise and fall of her breasts which she was trying and failing to hide. 'I had another woman in my arms only yesterday,' he repeated slowly.

'The woman in the gold bikini!' she accused, hating the shaft of pure jealousy which shot through her.

'The woman in the gold bikini?'

'Will you stop repeating everything I say?'

'Then would you mind explaining what the hell you're talking about?'

'The gold bikini top,' elaborated Kat bitterly. 'The one I found along with the remains of the meal in the dining room!'

'Ah, yes!' A slow and glittering smile of comprehension began to curve at Carlos's lips as he remembered. 'Tania Stephens...I had forgotten all about that.'

Kat felt sick, appalled at her own behaviour. She had been...been... Well, if she were being absolutely honest, hadn't she been like the softest putty in his hands? Wouldn't she still be writhing pleasurably beneath his practised caresses if he hadn't put a stop to it so abruptly? And yet he'd been doing the same thing to another woman only yesterday and had *forgotten all about it*! Didn't that speak volumes about his attitude to women in general and her in particular? What a lucky escape she had had!

'You make love to a woman and less than twenty-four hours later you've "forgotten all about it"?' she breathed in disbelief.

'I did not make love to her.'

Kat's heart pounded. 'So a woman's gold bikini top just *happens* to be lying discarded on the floor of your dining room, along with evidence of some intimate little meal *à deux*—and yet you claim to know nothing about it?'

'That's not what I said,' he snapped. 'I said that I didn't make love to her.'

'But…but she wanted to?'

There was a pause. 'Of course she did,' he agreed softly. 'All women want me to make love to them. Didn't you demonstrate that yourself only moments ago?'

Kat flinched at the accusation, but she couldn't deny it, could she? 'So who was she?' she questioned.

'A journalist.' Carlos allowed himself a brief, hard smile. 'Who I heard was doing a feature on me—and so I invited her here to find out what angle she was taking, and whether or not I needed to persuade her to adopt a different one.'

'Why would anyone want to do a feature on you?'

Black eyes challenged her. 'Any ideas?'

'Because you're rich? Or because you're unbearable?'

He gave a soft laugh. 'Wealth is hardly an achievement in its own right. You of all people should know that, *Princesa*.'

And then she remembered the photo. That startling photo. The young Carlos wearing the richly ornate jacket of the bullfighter—his face just as proud and as beautiful as it was now, but without the cynicism which time had etched onto the features of his older self.

'Bullfighting,' she said slowly. 'She wanted to talk to you about bullfighting.'

There was the beat of a pause. 'Of course she did,' he said slowly. 'They always want to talk about bullfighting.'

'But why?' Kat stared at him. 'Because it's exciting—or because hardly anyone does it as a career choice?'

'Both those things, but it is a little more complex than that.' He met the question in her eyes. 'It's fifteen years since I left the ring, and she's just digging around because she wants to know why.'

'And why did you leave?'

'You think I want to talk about it with someone like you?' he queried softly. 'A woman whose definition of a hard day's work is painting her own nails because the manicurist happens to be off sick?'

He saw her flinch but Carlos didn't care. Couldn't she take the truth about the kind of woman she was? He had vowed never to talk of those days, to relive the pain and the torture which had raged inside him during his tumultuous years in the ring. A pain which had little to do with the noble bullfight itself, and more to do with the cruel father who had made his life such a torment.

The journalist had tried every trick in the book to get him to talk, and a couple more besides. She had certainly been enterprising, he would say that for her. The editor had probably selected her for her beauty and her sheer ruthlessness. So that when the lunchtime interview had not been progressing as she'd wished, she had suggested sunbathing.

And then laughingly stripped off her bikini top as if it had been the most natural thing in the world.

He had been aroused, yes—of course he had. The woman's breasts had been full and pale and her glossy lips had parted as if to demonstrate that she was very accomplished with her mouth. But sex offered to him on a plate had never been his thing.

He looked down into the blue eyes of the Balfour girl. Maybe he should tell *her* that and have done with it—because, in effect, wasn't she doing exactly the same? Trying to twist him round her little finger with her come-to-bed eyes and pouting lips. Perhaps he should tell her that no matter how much she tried to tempt him, she was here to do a job and nothing more. He had given his word to her father that he would teach her something in the way of commitment, and Carlos always kept his word.

So why had he kissed her? And why was the memory of that kiss making him grow hard even now? So hard that he would have liked to have taken hold of her aristocratic hips and thrust right into her.

'You'd better have some breakfast,' he said harshly. 'And then start by clearing away the mess in the dining room.'

Kat met the stony black gaze. 'And if I don't?'

He thought how beautiful she looked when she defied him. 'If you don't? Then, *Princesa*, I will quickly lose patience with you, and I don't think that's such a good idea,' he answered. 'You might do well to remember that the sooner you start fulfilling your obligations, the sooner you can leave—and free us both from this infernal incarceration.'

Shaken, Kat stood watching as he walked away from her, her eyes drawn to the graceful movement of his white-jeaned physique and the way the silk shirt billowed slightly in the breeze. Unthinkingly, she touched her fingertips to her lips—to where the tender flesh still tingled with the heat of his passionate kiss—and she felt the corresponding thunder of her heart as she remembered it. But the kiss meant *nothing,* she reminded herself—and Carlos couldn't have made that clearer.

She wondered if he'd gone off to work in one of the warren of luxurious rooms which lay below the deck, but it wasn't until a few minutes later when she heard the throaty roar of a powerful engine that she realised that he'd gone. Properly gone.

Racing over to the side of the yacht, she saw a flash of silver as a powerful little motorboat cut through the sapphire waters. The wind streamed through the wild black curls of the man who stood at the helm and the sun had illuminated his olive skin into dark gold. He looked, she thought, like some powerful and formidable god of a man.

For one split second, their eyes met—and Kat registered the implacable coldness in his gaze, with barely a flicker of recognition or acknowledgement on his stony features. Was he demonstrating the fact that he was free to come and go as she was not? Or was he silently laughing at her and her lowly predicament?

She turned away and looked around the deck. Either way, she was trapped here—with a list of menial chores to do for a sexy tyrant of a man, and no means by which she could escape.

CHAPTER FIVE

AFTER Carlos had gone, Kat was left with the stinging realisation that she'd never had to clean up after anyone.

At all the different schools she'd attended—before being kicked out of most of them—there had always been someone else to make the beds and do the laundry for the privileged schoolgirls. Even at home, she'd managed to wriggle out of helping with domestic chores—maybe because her kindly and efficient mother had been a bit of a pushover.

When her mother had divorced Oscar and married Victor, it had been a fairly amicable arrangement for all concerned. But even so, Tilly Balfour had been so racked with guilt over the inevitable disruption it had caused that she'd tried to cushion her three daughters against any emotional fallout by spoiling them just a little. And Kat, being the youngest, had been very easy to spoil.

And then when Tilly's new husband had been posted to Sri Lanka, there had been servants galore to run around after the whole family. Until…

Kat blinked back the tears which could still catch her by surprise, even all these years later. But for once the thought was stubbornly refusing to be blocked.

When Victor had been killed—murdered—nobody in their right mind was going to ask Kat to do anything she didn't want to do. And if they did, then she usually turned her back on it and ran away.

But now suddenly that had all changed. Because for the first time in her life—quite literally—there was nowhere for her to run. And she was faced with a man she could not twist around her little finger. A man she still desired, no matter how much she tried to deny it.

She felt the acrid rise of panic in her throat—but with an effort she forced herself to crush it because what good would panicking do? It would paralyse her as much as stubborn defiance, and she could afford to do neither. Because even though she hated to admit it, she could see that if she wanted to get off this boat she was going to have to make some kind of an effort. To *co-operate* with Carlos Guerrero, even though every fibre of her being screamed out in protest.

Kat set off to explore the galley, where she found a cupboard containing an army of brushes, buckets and cloths as well as a confusing array of cleaning products, and she carried a selection of these down into the dining salon and set to work.

The first thing she did was to dispose of the gold bikini top, gingerly picking it up as if it was contaminated and chucking it into a black bin-liner. With a smile of satisfaction on her lips, she threw all the left-over food on top of it and watched the gleaming fabric sink beneath the weight of a banana skin. After that, she piled up all the crockery and china onto a tray and carried the whole lot down into the galley, and left it by the side of the sink before going back upstairs.

With the table now clear, she gave the place a quick wipe and sprayed some furniture polish in the air for added effect because she remembered reading somewhere that this would make the room *smell* clean. And then, her tasks completed and with no sign of Carlos returning from his boat trip, she slipped into a bikini of her own, found a magazine and went to lie by the swimming pool.

It should have been heaven basking there—with the warmth of the sun stealing over her skin and the sound of the waves swishing rhythmically against the boat. But in truth, Kat felt jittery and couldn't concentrate on any of the iconic fashion images which usually held her attention—because a face with glittering black eyes and a mocking stare kept breaking into her thoughts and unsettling her.

She did her best to enjoy the hours which drifted by and eventually fell into a fitful sleep—only jumping into half wakefulness by the sound of a distant drone and then by the certainty that someone was watching her. Her eyes fluttered open to see that her thoughts had become reality and a shadow had fallen over her—its hard, dark outline making her heart leap into an annoyingly dizzy and familiar beat. Kat felt her throat dry. Carlos!

'What the hell do you think you're doing?' came a low and disbelieving voice.

She'd tidied up his salon, hadn't she? Put on that stupid apron and buzzed around like Mrs Mop? Yanking the straps of her bikini back up, she sat up and pushed the hair away from her face. 'What does it look like?'

'It looks,' he gritted out, trying very hard not to let his gaze linger on the miniscule bikini she was wearing, 'as if you're just indulging in a little more of the same of your idle, jet-set lifestyle.'

'I've done what you asked me to do!'

'Oh, really?' he questioned dangerously.

'Yes, really,' she defended. 'I've tidied up the mess left by you and your tame journalist—'

'You think so? Then I must beg to differ, *Princesa*. You've left it only half done,' he corrected coldly. 'The salon is not properly clean and I understand you haven't even bothered to wash up.'

'So?'

'So, you'd better get it into that little air-brain head of yours that I am used to perfection from my staff and you have fallen way short of that. And what about the crew's lunch?'

'What about it?'

'It's almost three o'clock. Didn't it occur to you that they might be hungry?'

Three o' clock? Kat stared at him blankly. 'Is it really *that* time?' she queried. 'I had no idea—and as you know, my watch is broken—'

'Get up when you're talking to me!' he roared, and then when, to his surprise, she shrugged and began effortlessly to rise like some graceful Venus emerging from a shell, he instantly regretted his suggestion.

Because if he'd thought that the little sundress she'd been sashaying around in earlier was sinful, then this bikini was positively X-rated. *¡Madre de Dios!* Two tiny scraps of turquoise material which had been sewn with exquisite care to make a garment which was only this side of decent. Or maybe it was just the way she wore it. Her breasts seemed to be spilling over a woefully inadequate top and the bikini bottoms taunted him with two tantalising bows on either side of her hips. Bows which could be undone with a single tug of a silken piece of fabric….

Bad enough that her kiss had awoken in him an inconvenient hunger he had no intention of satisfying, but to add fuel to the fire which still smouldered within him, he was now forced to confront the stuff of fantasy.

'And for pity's sake, cover yourself up!' he snapped. 'Instead of draping yourself around the deck like some kind of latter-day Mata Hari!'

'Who?'

'It doesn't matter,' he retorted impatiently, tossing her a filmy sarong. 'Put this on?'

With a scowl, Kat folded and weaved the piece of material around herself, pushing her feet into a pair of glittery flip-flops. 'So what do you want me to do now?' she questioned insolently.

To his fury Carlos felt the sudden hot rush of blood to his groin. Thinking that if she'd asked any other man such a question in such circumstances as these, she might find herself being pushed back on that sun lounger and having the turquoise bikini peeled away from her body. And this time he just might not have the self-control to stop....

Carlos swallowed down the dryness in his throat. 'Just go and get dressed,' he ordered tersely. 'And then come back here.'

Infuriated by his peremptory tone, Kat was tempted to disobey him just for the hell of it, but the rebellion had left her by the time she reached her cabin. Because hadn't she already decided that there was no point in fighting him—other than an enduring battle of wills which Carlos would surely win, simply because he was in the dominant position of power? No. Better to co-operate. To make an attempt to do the wretched man's bidding and pray that time passed quickly.

Peeling off her bikini, she changed into a pair of linen trousers and T-shirt. She even twisted the thick fall of her dark hair into a practical knot and pulled on the dreaded apron, regarding her reflection in the mirror with a grimace. Why, she was scarcely recognisable as herself!

He was waiting where she'd left him, talking into a cellphone, his dark features shuttered as he finished his conversation.

'Buy,' he was saying softly. 'But don't go any higher than forty. *No. No. De eso ni hablar. Sí.*'

He glanced up as Kat approached, his black eyes narrowing as he terminated the connection, surprised to see that she had fallen in completely with his wishes and had covered up. The turquoise bikini had been consigned to fevered memory, but although almost every centimetre of her flesh was no longer visible, her outfit did little to deter the heated progression of his thoughts.

She should have looked demure, but somehow she failed on every level because now he knew only too well what lay beneath. He could picture her creamy-caramel flesh beautifully naked, with all its enticing shadows which beckoned a man to the places where nature had intended for him to linger. The firm curve of buttock and breast, and the delicious honey-sweet destination between her thighs.

'Is that better?' asked Kat.

'Marginally better,' he conceded thickly.

'What were you buying on the phone just now?'

'Property.'

'Is that what you do, then?'

'Some of what I do. And stop trying to change the subject. Just go back down to the galley and wash up all the dishes which I'm told you left dumped on the side. And after that, you can make a start on dinner. Do you think you can manage that?'

The fact that he obviously *didn't* think she could rankled, and a long-forgotten streak of pride made Kat nod her head. How difficult could it be to knock up a meal? 'Of course I can manage,' she said haughtily.

But once she'd made her way downstairs, Kat found herself wondering just what she had agreed to. What the hell could she cook for seven hungry men, including one she knew would be exacting and waiting to take her to task if she made the slightest mistake? Especially as she'd never cooked a meal for anyone in her life.

She thought back to all the different restaurants she'd eaten in over the years. Surely one of those could give her a bit of inspiration? What about that amazing, award-winning place in the centre of Paris, where they'd served a whole duck smothered with a delicious, creamy sauce and everyone around the table had sighed in delight? Couldn't she do the same sort of thing with the giant fish which was currently wrapped in newspaper at the back of the fridge and which, according to Mike, had been bought from a passing fishing boat that very morning? Perhaps with some sort of salad to start, leaving room for the elaborate kind of pudding which all men seemed to love?

But events seemed to be conspiring against her, even though she attempted to use the remaining hours as constructively as possible. The oven took some getting used to—and in between all the juggling of ingredients and familiarizing herself with an astonishingly large store cupboard, there was still the table to lay.

'Where does Carlos usually eat?' she asked Mike distractedly.

'It varies,' answered Mike, snapping open a can of cold cola and then swallowing half of it. 'Sometimes with us, sometimes up on deck. Depends if he's working—usually he has some big deal on and rarely comes up for air, and it's best to leave him be. He's…well, he's a bit of a loner.' The engineer shrugged, and smiled. 'But when he eats with the crew—well, he's pretty laid-back.'

Kat didn't respond to that. Personally, she found Carlos Guerrero about as laid-back as a piranha fish. but she was not going to let her own feelings ruin what she was determined was going to be a fantastic meal.

'He seems to want breakfast at the crack of dawn—and my watch is broken,' she said slowly.

'Don't worry,' said Mike. 'I can lend you an alarm clock if it helps. He's dead hot on punctuality.'

Kat grimaced. 'So I gather.'

The evening didn't start very promisingly. All her timings were out so that the fish was cooked before the starter was even ready, the sauce she'd cobbled together had started to curdle and she forgot all about the accompanying vegetables until the last minute. With a grimace she lifted up the lid of the boiling potatoes—only for a cloud of steam to hit her in the face and make her feel as if she'd been thrown into a sauna.

There wasn't even enough time for her to touch up her make-up and brush her hair before the hungry crew arrived. They crowded in a cluster around the table outside, onto which she'd just piled a haphazard collection of crockery and glasses.

And then Carlos appeared, looking infuriatingly cool and sexy. *He* had clearly found time to shower and change because the thick black hair was still damp and Kat thought she could detect the raw clean tang of sandalwood.

For a moment he just stood there, surveying the general air of disarray—and his mouth twisted.

'Has someone trashed the boat while I've been showering, or are you trying to sabotage the meal in order to prove a point, *Princesa*?'

An image of Carlos in the shower was the last thing Kat needed to add to her already-shot nerves, and a renewed waft of sandalwood as he waved a disparaging arm around didn't help. She gritted her teeth in a grim replica of a smile. 'Would…would you like to sit down?'

'Where?' he questioned pointedly.

Kat leant over and cleared a space at the table. 'Right there. Dinner is about to be served.'

'I can hardly wait.'

Horrible, sarcastic *tyrant*! I'll show him, vowed Kat silently, as she went back into the cramped galley to prod at a boiling potato which unfortunately still had the consistency of a rock. She tipped salad onto eight plates and drizzled on some of the dressing she'd made, trying desperately to remember what was supposed to go in it, but afraid to ask for fear of looking stupid.

But she knew the moment that everyone had started eating that something was wrong.

'Is everything…okay?' she questioned.

There was a brief but loaded silence.

'Salad dressing which tastes of washing-up liquid is an interesting innovation, *querida*, but perhaps it's easy to see why it hasn't yet come to dominate the market,' came Carlos's sarcastic assessment, and Kat felt like hurling a dish at his arrogant face as the rest of the crew burst into relieved laughter and pushed their barely touched plates away.

The main course was no better. The fish was stone-cold, the potatoes still rock-hard and the overambitious sauce had congealed into a horrible mess around the plate. As

Carlos pointed out, it was a waste of a perfectly good fish, and once again Kat ended up scraping most of it into the garbage.

She felt hot from the heat of the kitchen when she appeared on deck again after crushing amaretto biscuits and cooking some mixed berries which now resembled roadkill. They looked up at her expectantly. Seven faces in all, but Kat could see only one. It swam before her line of vision with cold ebony eyes that mocked her which made her aware that her face must be flushed and her hair falling down.

'Everyone ready for pudding?'

'What kind of pudding?' questioned Mike.

'I'm calling it "Berry Surprise",' said Kat brightly.

Carlos took a mouthful of wine and put his glass down, a sardonic smile curving the edges of his lips. 'Please, no more surprises—not tonight—I don't think I could take it.' There was an answering peal of laughter from the other men before he fixed her with a cool stare. 'I don't really think you're up to it—at least, not tonight. Perhaps you could bring some cheese and fruit upstairs and I'll eat there instead.'

She wanted to tell him to get it himself. That she wasn't his slave. But in a way, that's exactly what she *was*. And if she threw some sort of tantrum about her treatment, wouldn't that only increase his glaring contempt for her?

And stupidly, his assessment hurt. Really hurt. *I don't really think you're up to it.* With those few wounding words he had made her feel so…so *inferior.* And the trouble was that he had been right. Was he a man who enjoyed wounding, she wondered bitterly, and was that why he had been such a success as a bullfighter?

Determined to salvage something of the evening, Kat put a ridiculous amount of care into arranging a dish for him, washing and drying all the fruit and arranging it in an artful rainbow display. Placing two pieces of cheese at the dish's centre, she added bread and crackers and took it upstairs, to a deck that was washed with moonlight and empty save for a tall figure which dominated the skyline.

Carlos was leaning over the rail, looking out to sea—and there was something so silent and imposing about his frozen stance that, for a moment, Kat just stood in the shadows silently watching him. Seemingly lost in thought, she'd never seen anyone looking quite so *alone* before—nor quite so comfortable with his own sense of solitude.

And despite his wounding words, she found herself realising that she knew little of the man who was now effectively her employer. Not even how old he was. Mid-thirties, perhaps— maybe more, for his handsome face was hard and lined with experience and he carried with him a habitual and faint air of cynicism. Why hadn't he settled down with a wife and a family, she wondered, when women must have been beating a path to his door for most of his adult life? Was it because, as Mike had said, he was a true loner?

He must have heard her, or sensed her presence, because he turned round and Kat forced herself to stir into life, to step out of the shadows and into his private circle of silver moonlight.

'I'll...I'll put this over here,' she said, holding the platter up, her voice suddenly faltering and she wasn't sure why. 'Is that okay?'

'Thanks.'

He watched as she bent over the table, the

dark hair falling in untidy strands around her face and the linen she wore now looking crumpled. And yet she looked...*delicious*— more womanly than at any other time he'd seen her, and curiously accessible without her ridiculous high-fashion status symbols and dripping with jewels. Her face was flushed with heat and the effects of probably the only honest day's work she'd ever done.

How ironic that this sexy creature was as unlike the real Kat Balfour as it was possible to imagine.

Kat straightened up to find the ebony eyes fixed on her and, as she stared into the shadowed and shuttered features, her heart began a strange, rhythmical pounding. Nervously, her tongue flicked over her lips as she looked up into the impenetrable black eyes. 'Will...will there be anything else?'

Oh, what a question, he thought wryly. Innocent or deliberately provocative? Was she doing her best to slip into her role as domestic, or simply acknowledging the silent hunger which was sizzling between them? He felt the thud of his heart. As if sexy Kat Balfour would ever do innocence! 'No.

Nothing else.' He shook his head as he read the silent yearning on her face—was she mirroring something of his own, he wondered frustratedly.

She went to walk past him but something made him stop her. Something in the gleam of moonlight which glanced off the thick abundance of her dark hair and arrested his attention as much as the pure lines of her perfect profile and the parted promise of her soft lips.

He stayed her with a touch of his hand to her bare forearm and she looked down at it and then up at him and he could feel her shiver beneath him. Could feel an answering tremor in his own body—the familiar tightening, like a bow being stretched by the sharp point of the arrow.

'Kat,' he murmured, barely aware that he had said her name.

All Kat was aware of was the wild black buccaneer curls which framed the shuttered face. The way that the moonlight cast indigo shadows on the golden-olive skin. The powerful physique and the long, long legs. She swallowed. It was as if he had cast some dark and silken net over her, rendering her incapable of sensible thought and feeling. Making her world telescope down and focus on the vibrant allure of the Spaniard. He had done it unconsciously on the night of the Balfour Ball but now she was certain that he was doing it deliberately. Why? *Why?* Was he simply playing with her—as a cat played with a foolish mouse before it moved in for the careless kill?

'Stop it,' she whispered, hardly realising what she was saying.

'Stop what?' he echoed.

'Making me...' Embarrassed now, her words tailed off—for how could she possibly admit to him what she didn't even want to acknowledge to herself?

Yet it seemed that Carlos had no such similar qualms, for he gave her a mocking smile.

'Stop making you want me?' he taunted softly. 'But I'm not. You're doing that all by yourself. You just can't help yourself, can you, Kat?'

She shook her head, rooted to the spot as if he had turned her into a statue. Where was the wisecracking Kat now? The woman who was left cold by members of the opposite sex? 'Yes, I can,' she whispered, but even to her own ears the denial sounded phony.

'*Liar.*' His voice dipped to become a verbal caress. 'I can read your desire for me in your eyes—it's so obvious that you might as well be carrying a banner saying so. And I can see it in your lips too—their beautiful pout forgotten. Everything forgotten, in fact—because there's only one thing on your mind and we both know what that is.'

'Please!' Her protest came out like a squeak—and now she even *sounded* like a mouse. Was that because she couldn't bring herself to inject the word with any real conviction? Because despite Carlos's clear disdain for her on so many levels, she stupidly wanted him just as much as she'd always wanted him?

'You're longing for me to kiss you, aren't you, Kat?' he mused. 'To kiss you—only this time, not to stop. To lie you down and part your silken thighs and to thrust into you long and hard and deep until you cry out your pleasure.'

Kat's knees buckled and for a very real moment she was afraid that she might faint, because the graphic words were only increasing her desire. And how shameful was that? Tell him no. Tell him no and then push past him and go back down to the galley. He might be a practised seducer with a cruel tongue which could lash out at her, but she doubted that he would actually pull her into his arms and take her by *force*. Hating herself for the shiver of longing which accompanied this dark fantasy, Kat stayed mute.

'Aren't you?' he prompted silkily.

Her desire became intolerable. Unbearable. She fought and fought it but in the end it was no good. *'Yes!'* she burst out at last. 'Yes, I am!'

Carlos nodded, recognising what it must have cost her to admit it. 'Well, that makes two of us,' he said unsteadily, and leaned forward to kiss her unprotesting lips.

She had expected urgency. A rapid escalation into full-blown desire. An unashamed seduction. But Kat was wrong. Instead, he slowly pushed the fallen strands of hair away from her face as if he had all the time in the world, studying it like a scientist looking through a microscope for some rogue cell. He let his gaze drift from her brow to her eyes, then slowly down until it focused entirely upon her lips, and she felt them automatically part beneath his scrutiny.

'Flawless,' he said slowly, shaking his head a little. 'Absolutely flawless.'

The kiss, when it came, was nothing like she expected. More of a graze than a kiss—a quicksilver brush of his lips against hers. And then again. Back and forth his mouth teased her, light as a butterfly and as tantalising as the first warmth of the morning sun. His breath was warm and she could smell his own particular raw, clean scent. It was a kiss which managed to be both innocent and sensual all at the same time. Nothing more than that, but enough to make Kat sway and weaken.

'Oh!' she breathed, and hungrily she reached for him.

But, using an expertise which he'd employed more than most men—often to literally save his own skin in the bullring— Carlos neatly sidestepped the movement. Putting out his hand he caught and steadied her, though he kept his body at an untouchable distance from hers, his face tight with tension. Because this was, in a way, the ultimate demonstration of his formidable control over his body.

'No. *No.*' There was a moment while he steadied his breath, and when he spoke he seemed to be speaking to himself as much as to her. 'I can't do it,' he said flatly.

Incredulity made her voice falter even while her body screamed out for the closeness of his. 'C-can't?'

Carlos narrowed his eyes. Did the little witch think he was *incapable* of giving her what she wanted? 'Forgive me if I have not made myself clear, *Princesa.* Sometimes when I speak in English, the subtleties of your language escape me. What I should have said is that I *won't* make love to you.' Her bright blue eyes continued to stare at him in puzzled query. *Maldición*, but she was persistent. And shameless, he reminded himself. For a woman like this was used to getting exactly what she wanted—and she wanted him. Too bad. 'It would be an abuse of my role as your employer,' he finished softly.

The rejection hurt more than it should have done and the telltale pricking of her eyes warned her that she might be about to do something intolerable, like burst into tears. And that Mr Ego might think she was crying over *him*. As if she would ever shed a tear over a man as unfeeling as Carlos Guerrero!

But Kat knew she needed to get away from here—and quickly—before he inflicted any more emotional damage on her.

As she lifted her head with a proud gesture, she was grateful at that moment for all the poise which her years as a Balfour had taught her. All the showy affairs where she had learnt to put on a careless expression.

'You're probably right,' she said, and the surprised narrowing of his eyes gave her the courage to continue, even though her voice was threatening to tremble. 'Affairs in the work place are never a good idea, or so they tell me. So if you've got everything you want, I'll go downstairs and start clearing up.'

Just let him try to stop me, she thought fiercely, as she brushed past him. Just let him *try*.

But he didn't try. Although his shuttered black eyes were watchful, he let her go without a further word.

And frustration only increased her bitter

sense of rejection, as Kat half ran from the deck and back downstairs to the galley with tears blinding her eyes.

CHAPTER SIX

THE alarm clock shrilled out like a fire alarm and Kat woke with a start. Fumblingly, she switched it off and made herself get straight out of bed before she fell asleep again, surprised at how deeply she'd slept. And surprised that the restless night she'd anticipated hadn't materialised—despite the fact that Carlos had rejected her for a second time. Maybe because it had been past midnight when she'd finally crept to bed after clearing away the remains of the disastrous meal—and she'd been too tired to do anything but fall into a dreamless sleep.

Quickly, she showered, dressed and was on deck soon after six, determined to salvage something of her pride. She was *not* going to think of Carlos—or his teasing and provocative kisses and the fact that he seemed to like playing with her. As if it gave him some sort of kick to demonstrate his power over her. Kat stared out to sea, her lips set in a line of grim determination. What had happened couldn't be reversed, and this morning she was damned well going to show Señor Guerrero that she was worth something.

And despite the bizarre circumstances in which she found herself and her trepidation of what the day might bring, Kat couldn't deny the beauty of her surroundings as she stood quietly for a moment. The light was soft and milky, the sky tinged with rose and tangerine and the dark blue sea stretched towards the horizon as far as the eye could see.

Even the oven in the galley seemed like an old friend this morning so that she was able to warm the half-baked bread without mishap and assemble it on a tray with fruit and a pot of strong, dark coffee which she carried up just before seven, just as Carlos appeared, laptop under his arm.

Dressed in jeans and a soft silk shirt, his face was shuttered as he walked out onto the sun-washed deck—but the way he carried himself was so full of grace that just for a moment Kat was dazzled. How easily she could imagine him in the bullring—his head held proud and his narrow hips encased in those dark, tight breeches as he weaved a mystifying dance around a huge, quivering bull. *Stop it,* she told herself fiercely. *Stop fantasising about him.*

Hadn't she told herself that from now on she was going to remain immune to his dark beauty? That he had little respect for her as a person and had rejected her as a woman. So why was it that she seemed to be powerless over the thunder of her heart as she carried the tray towards the table?

'Good morning!' she said.

Carlos watched her approach and his eyes narrowed. There was something *different* about her this morning and he couldn't quite work out what it was. '*No me lo creo,*' he observed, his voice silky. 'I don't believe it. The *princesa* is up and working—and what is more…she's on time.'

Kat put the tray down. 'You said breakfast at seven and here it is—I'm simply following your orders, Carlos.'

'But I am impressed, *Princesa*. I was expecting sulky acquiescence.' And hadn't he thought that she might be a touch coquettish this morning, her body silently imploring him to carry on with what he'd so foolishly begun last night? Perhaps he had. But her attitude towards him was merely businesslike as she poured out a cup of coffee. *He* had been the one to suffer an agitated night spent trying to banish the memory of her soft kiss and eager body—and yet here *she* was, looking infuriatingly calm and rested. 'Not such an air of docile servility,' he finished softly.

'Docile servility wasn't what I was aiming for,' Kat returned. 'I'm just trying to do my job to the best of my ability since I seem to be stuck with it.'

'So what's the catch?' he questioned softly.

'Catch? No catch, Carlos. I've decided to accept my fate and do what's required of me.' She pushed the coffee across the table towards him. 'But I wanted to ask you a favour.'

'What kind of favour?'

Kat shrugged. 'Well, I can't possibly provide meals for the crew when I don't really know how to cook.'

'So what are you suggesting?' he drawled. 'That I fly out a trained chef to teach you how to boil an egg?'

'I think that even *I* could manage an egg. Actually, I was thinking of something a little simpler.'

'Such as?'

'Well, access to the Internet would help. I assume you have it on board?'

'Oh, come on.' His hard smile became edged with mockery. 'And have you sending out SOS messages to all the admiring men in your life, asking them to come and rescue you?'

Kat shook her head. The only man she could imagine masterminding some sort of high-seas rescue mission was sitting right in front of her and he was far from admiring. 'I'm not planning to escape. I already told you that. All I want is to find some simple recipes with simple instructions. Recipes that I might actually be able to use—and prevent some sort of mutiny from the crew.'

Carlos studied her thoughtfully. She had a point. There was no way he wanted a repeat of the fiasco they'd been forced to endure last evening. The question was—could he trust her? Should he even try? Staring down into her brilliant blue eyes, he dipped his voice. 'But if I let you, I don't want you wasting time.'

'Of course not.'

'No emails. No browsing unrelated web-sites.'

What a tyrant he was! 'Maybe you'd like to stand over me and police it?' she challenged.

He met the challenge in her eyes with one of his own. 'Maybe I will.' Or maybe it would be a little crazy to put temptation in his way when he was finding it harder and harder to remain immune to her aristocratic appeal.

Sipping his coffee, he studied her. This morning she'd tied the thick black hair back into a single plump plait which gave her a particularly youthful appearance—emphasised by the simple shorts, T-shirt and deck shoes she wore. But it was something else. Something other than a more casual look than she usually favoured. He frowned. 'You're not wearing any make-up,' he observed slowly.

With something of a shock, Kat lifted her fingertips to her face as she realised that he was right—and that she hadn't even noticed. She who had worn make-up every day since she'd been fifteen years old! 'There wasn't time this morning. To be honest I didn't even think about it. I…I must look a fright.'

A fright? He felt the sudden beating of a pulse at his temple and the flickering throb of awareness as their eyes met. 'On the contrary— I think it suits you,' he said obliquely, pleased when his cellphone began to ring and he could turn his back on the crushed-petal perfection of her lips. 'Speak to Mike about the Internet— tell him I've given you permission to have limited access. And I mean *limited*, *Princesa*.'

He really *was* a control freak, Kat thought, as she heard him begin to speak rapidly in Spanish, and she hurried down to the galley to make herself a cup of coffee.

But the tiny freedom Carlos had granted her by allowing her access to the Internet somehow shifted the balance of power, if only slightly. Very subtly it changed her attitude towards her enforced captivity. By giving her an element of responsibility, she now felt that she had something to prove to him—and she was determined to do it.

She was allocated use of the desktop computer in Carlos's study which apparently he used mainly in winter or when the weather was inclement. His desk was bare and uncluttered—without a single family photo and barely a keepsake which might have given a clue about the identity of its owner. Only a single oil painting gave some sort of idea about what kind of life Carlos Guerrero might live when he wasn't at sea—and it was not what Kat would have expected. Instead of some sophisticated modern canvas, the painting was of a lovely and rather old-fashioned house set in a beautiful landscape of lemon trees and distant mountains, bounded by a sky which was vast and magnificent.

Kat found herself staring at it more than once and wondering where it was—and if it had been anyone else she might have asked them. But not Carlos. Carlos didn't really invite small talk—and hadn't he made it crystal clear that any kind of personal interaction between the two of them was strictly off the menu?

She found a website for beginner cooks called 'Can't Boil An Egg?' which was reader-friendly and took her through all the basics. And Kat soon realised that the number-one rule about successful cooking was to keep it simple. Fancy sauces and hundreds of clashing ingredients were passé—fresh and seasonal was the way to go.

She soon found that the stronger she made the coffee, the more everyone liked it—Carlos especially. And that the crew adored warm bread served with every meal, and were just as happy with cheese as a pudding afterwards.

That wasn't to say that there were no more disasters, though none quite as bad as on that first night. She quickly learnt that it was a mistake to make ice cream unless you were a lot more experienced than she was. And Kat soon noticed a direct correlation between hard work and personal satisfaction. That if the crew—and Carlos—were happy with the meals she prepared, then she was too….

Happy? Well, that might not be the best word to choose to describe her feelings, not when she felt a sense of aching awareness every time she saw him. The memory of his kiss lingered just as potently in her mind as it ever had and reminded her how it felt to be held close to that powerful, hard body. And she'd have been a liar if she'd denied her desire to have him pull her into his arms again—only this time, not to stop. To carry on plundering her lips with that hard and hungry kiss…

She was just writing down a recipe for a green sauce to accompany some free-range chickens she'd defrosted when a shadow fell over the desk and she looked up to find Carlos standing there staring down at her, his expression inscrutable.

'How diligently you work, *Princesa*,' he said softly.

Hating herself for noticing that the top three buttons of his shirt were revealing a tantalising triangle of silken olive-gold flesh, Kat attempted an expression of cool efficiency. Not easy when her heart was pounding so loudly beneath her breast that she was surprised he hadn't heard it.

'Is that supposed to be a criticism?'

'Actually, it was supposed to be a compliment.'

'In that case…thank you.'

'You're welcome,' he mocked.

Walking over to a line of leather-bound books, he ran his forefinger over the ornate gold script of an atlas, trying to analyse why he found Kat Balfour's presence here so unsettling. Maybe because a boat was such a confined space and he was not used to being in such close proximity to a woman—not 24/7. It was too close to something Carlos didn't do—and that something was intimacy.

Because Carlos compartmentalised his women, in the same way that he compartmentalised the rest of his life. Work came first—which was why he now owned real estate in most of the major capital cities in Europe. He rarely took a holiday—even his luxury yacht doubled as a temporary office when he was on board. Enforced relaxation made him restless—it always had.

Women were for bedding and occasionally providing a little light relief in his high-powered competitive world. The occasional dinner or breakfast with them he could tolerate, mainly because he knew that was the price you paid for sex. But the moment they started yearning for the impossible—some kind of commitment—then that was the time to kiss them goodbye. With a costly bauble which would cushion some of the pain they felt on parting.

But having Kat here…

He wondered if she knew just how different she looked from the pouting beauty who'd arrived. The absence of make-up seemed to have become a daily habit, just as she'd taken to wearing her clothes looking like she wanted to leave them on, instead of stripping them off to the sound of sultry music. Even her hair was now worn in a functional plait which fell over one shoulder.

The look should have been the antithesis of sexy, and yet ironically it was the very opposite. She looked very sexy indeed. Cinderella in reverse, Carlos thought wryly. And as she peeled off all the different layers of artifice, he thought he could catch a glimpse of the woman beneath.

'We were thinking of taking a couple of boats over to Capraia tonight,' he said suddenly.

'Capraia?' She blinked up at him. 'What's that?'

'A beautiful little island where you can eat

fish which has been caught about an hour previously. Want to come? We're all going.'

Kat nodded, not wanting to appear too eager. She told herself it was nothing but a careless query and yet she felt an unmistakable fizz of excitement. Dinner—with Carlos! Okay, the rest of the crew would be there too, but who cared? Automatically, she tugged at the thick plait which dangled over her shoulder. 'What time?'

'We'll leave at seven.' Black eyes flicked over her as he thought about all the unsuitable little outfits she might choose to send the other diners' blood pressure soaring. And his own. 'Oh, and don't bother getting dressed up and making some sort of fashion statement,' he said curtly. 'It's a casual little place.'

Kat heard the unmistakable censure in his voice as he walked out of the study, leaving her staring blankly at the computer screen, wondering what on earth would win such an exacting man's approval. Then she tried telling herself that she was dressing for herself—and not for anybody else.

But more than anything she wanted to fit in. To just be part of the gang—the way she'd never been before. Later that afternoon, she washed her hair and knotted it into a French plait, then changed into a simple white linen shift dress and a pair of brown leather gladiator sandals. Her face was naturally tanned, glowing from hard work and plenty of sleep and, she realised, didn't actually *need* any make-up.

She was aware of Carlos's eyes on her as she walked out on deck—and of his piercing black scrutiny as she stepped into the first boat. This was crazy, she thought faintly—they were surrounded by Mike and the others and yet she felt as self-conscious as if she were alone on a deserted beach with him.

The tiny island was a stunning pearl of a place, studded into a sea of matchless blue. Lots of different little boats bobbed around in the small harbour and the air was scented with sweet local herbs which perfumed the air the moment they stepped ashore.

Kat found herself praying that she would be seated somewhere—anywhere—as long as it was away from Carlos and his watchful black eyes. Then felt the thrill of unalloyed pleasure when he slid his long-legged form onto the narrow bench opposite her.

'Like it?' he questioned idly.

Drinking in the beauty of his rugged face, Kat smiled. 'What's not to like?' she said softly.

Hidden by the darkness of his sunglasses, Carlos ran his eyes over her, thinking that he had never seen her looking quite so relaxed or so carefree before. The simple dress suited her—it showed off the sleek lines of her limbs. His gaze drifted to her lips, wondering how, without any gloss or colour, they still managed to symbolise a kind of wanton wildness. Especially when they parted like that....

'Let's have some wine,' he said unevenly.

The waitress brought jugs of cold, red local wine to accompany the fish which they ate with rice flavoured with lentisk—an aromatic herb which Carlos told her grew prolifically on the island.

Kat put her fork down. 'My mother would probably have heard of it.'

Black eyes narrowed. 'Because?'

'Well, that's her job. She's a cook.'

He put his fork down. 'Your mother is a *professional cook*?'

'Yes, Carlos, my mother is a cook—she runs a small bakery business. You sound surprised.'

'Maybe that's because I am, *Princesa*.'

'You thought I'd been born with a silver spoon in my mouth?'

Thinking about her mouth again was a distraction he *didn't* need. 'Something like that.' Carlos frowned—because, yes, he'd imagined her to have been descended from a long line of aristocrats on both sides of her family. 'Your mother was Oscar's third wife, right?'

'Second,' said Kat drily. 'He's a much-married man, my father.'

He drank a mouthful of wine. 'And she was a cook when they met?'

'Well, not exactly. My mother was the family nanny. She worked for my father and his first wife, Alexandra, and looked after their three daughters. Then, when Alexandra died, he…well, it was hard for a man in his position to cope with a young family, especially in those days. He decided that he needed to get married again—and quickly. And since my mother already got on so well with his three girls—and with him—it seemed convenient for them to get married.'

'Convenient?' echoed Carlos sardonically as he speared a piece of fish and ate it.

Kat nodded. It wasn't a romantic way to describe a marriage, but her parents' union had never been a love match—and they had never pretended it had been. Inevitably, the relationship had become a self-fulfilling prophesy which had resulted in divorce. But at least the marital breakdown had been amicable—more amicable than anyone else's she knew. 'And they went on to have three daughters of their own. I'm one of them,' she added helpfully, because people always got thoroughly confused by Oscar's complicated love life.

'But no son?'

'No, no son.' She saw the look in his eyes. 'I suppose you think it's a tragedy not to have an heir?'

He shrugged. 'Well, yes. I would want an heir,' he said simply.

That didn't surprise her. But then, none of his outrageously macho behaviour really surprised her. Kat ate some fish, but the evening was much too balmy to produce an appetite. Plus, she wasn't finding it very easy to concentrate on food, not when Carlos was sitting there with the light breeze billowing at his silk shirt and hinting at the hard torso beneath. She pushed her plate away.

'Not hungry?' he questioned softly.

'Not really, no. It's too hot.'

'*Sí.*' Carlos leaned back in his chair. It was much too hot, and she was much too distracting. The sun was dipping now—its magnificent light gilding the deep sapphire of the sea, while the faint pinprick of stars were beginning to appear in the darkening sky. He could hear the slick lick of water as it slapped against the sides of the boats which were moored in the tiny port, and his eyes drank in the distant green hues of the island's mountains. It looked like paradise—and in truth, at that moment, it *felt* like paradise. Good food. Good wine—and a beautiful woman who wanted him. And if it were any other beautiful woman than Kat, he would be sailing urgently back to his yacht to make love to her.

His thoughts were rewarded with the sharp stab of desire and he cursed himself for his stupidity in dwelling on such thoughts. Because this was the real world, he reminded himself—not some soft-focus ad man's version of it.

Okay, so she'd embraced a little domesticity these past few days at sea, had shown that she wasn't completely spoiled. But she was still trouble. Still the kind of idle, rich woman for whom he had no time. The fact that he wanted her was just nature's idea of a joke—and nature could be cruel. Carlos's mouth hardened. Didn't he know that better than anyone?

He hadn't had sex in almost a year, although offers spoken and unspoken came his way pretty much every day of the week. But he was discerning—and increasingly so as time went by. Although creamy, firm flesh still appealed to him on a very base level, his boredom tolerance was at an all-time low. And sometime last year he had decided he couldn't face any more early morning pillow talk with beauties who turned out to be total airheads with nothing but marriage in mind.

Sooner or later he would carefully select for himself a bride with all the qualities he admired in a woman. Qualities such as humility and compassion. And she would possess a quiet, soft beauty—not the hard-edged glamour of this Balfour heiress.

So get away from her before the moon rises and the wine blurs your senses any more.

'Has everyone finished?' questioned Carlos, pulling a wallet from the back pocket of his jeans.

Deliberately, he sailed back in a different boat to Kat in an attempt to limit temptation to a manageable degree, though the two vessels were close enough for him to see her face as they cut through the indigo waters.

From the distant shore, he heard the crack-crack of some small explosion—was it fireworks?—and his attention was drawn to the small sound of alarm she made in response. Saw the sudden blanching of her face beneath her tan. Was she frightened of fireworks? he wondered.

But Kat Balfour's neuroses were as meaningless to him as was fantasising about her body.

She was there to work, Carlos thought grimly, as he turned his back to the other boat. Not to tempt him into doing something he would bitterly regret.

CHAPTER SEVEN

'No!'

The piercing and blood-curdling scream echoed through the night and Carlos woke instantly. Staring into the pitch darkness, his senses were on instant alert as the reality hit him that it was a woman's scream—and there was only one woman on board. He frowned. Kat? *Screaming?* What the hell was she playing at?

Leaping naked from his bed, he dragged on a pair of jeans and headed for her cabin, his heart pounding frantically in his chest as he pushed open the door.

'No!'

Once more he heard the terrified word torn from her throat as he burst inside—but it was not directed at him, nor at anyone else. For the cabin was empty save for Kat sitting bolt upright in bed. Through the moonlight which flooded in from the porthole he could see that her face was ashen with terror, her eyes glazed as they stared unseeingly in front of her. She looked as if she'd seen a ghost and was clearly having some kind of nightmare.

His movements were soft and stealthy as he moved towards her—remembering reading somewhere that if you startled someone from a nightmare, it could cause them a serious shock to the system.

'No, no, *no!*' she screamed again, now shaking her head wildly from side to side.

Carlos reached the bed and, brushing aside the silken spill of her hair, placed his hands on her shoulders, his voice as soothing as if he were calming down a fractious horse. He could feel the heat of her skin and see the frantic movement of a pulse at her temple. 'Kat,' he urged softly. 'Kat. Wake up. Come on, wake up, *Princesa*—you're having a bad dream.'

'No, *please*,' she whimpered. 'Please don't. Don't…'

He found her helpless whisper curiously affecting and a rush of unwilling protectiveness flared through him. Had someone attacked her in the past? Made her…

'Kat,' he said again, his voice firmer now. 'It's okay. You're here. Nothing's happened. Wake up. You're safe.'

Safe… The single word filtered into her consciousness as Kat awoke, memories which she kept buried deep and out of sight now staining her mind like a dark poison. Convulsively, she shivered as graphic images danced in her mind and sheer horror racked through her body.

But someone was holding her in their arms—and it was the warmest and most comfortable place she had ever been. So that, yes, for a moment, the word had the ring of truth to it and she really *did* feel safe. Safe and protected.

Until past and present merged with horrifying clarity. It was no nightmare. It *had* happened. Victor *was* dead. Her beloved stepfather gone.

'No,' she whimpered.

'Kat,' came a whisper as strong hands now shook her with surprising gentleness and her eyelids fluttered open. 'Wake *up*. Come on, wake up, *Princesa*.'

Her vision cleared and her heart missed a beat. Because the man holding her was none other than Carlos—sitting in *her* cabin and on *her* bed and wearing nothing but a pair of jeans.

The same man who had made it very clear he didn't want her was holding her in his arms—and Kat knew she should have torn herself away from his embrace and told him to go. What had she told herself about pride and not letting him see her vulnerable again? But she was still scared enough from the aftermath of the dream to want to stay exactly where she was. Here, where she could feel the powerful pound of his heart.

Carlos stroked the silken tumble of her hair, knowing that the rhythmical movement would soothe her, in the same way that frightened animals were always soothed by rhythm. He was aware of her sweetly scented femininity—but at least she wasn't distractingly naked. In fact, he was slightly taken aback by her choice of night attire, because a pair of cotton pyjamas was not what he might have expected the sexy Kat Balfour to sleep in.

'You were having a bad dream,' he stated softly.

Briefly closing her eyes, she shuddered. 'Yes.'

'Well, you're awake now, so forget it. Come on. Let it go. Nightmares don't happen in real life.'

Was it reaction to the shock of having the reoccurring dream that made her want to contradict him? Or was it because, with Carlos holding her like that, she felt as if nothing or no one could ever hurt her again?

'It's…it's n-not a n-nightmare.' Her voice was shaking with fear as she spoke against the silken warmth of his bare shoulder. 'It's t-true.'

Carlos knew about fear. After all, that was one of the simple lures of bullfighting. That's what the spectators paid huge amounts of money to witness. Why poor men would happily forgo half a week's wages to watch the ancient battle between man and bull. It had been a long time since he had encountered real fear outside the ring, but he could sense it now in the slender frame of this woman in his arms, and he stilled. 'What are you talking about?'

Lifting her cheek away from his shoulder, she looked up at him, her heart pounding as she met the gleam of his eyes which was as bright as the light of the moon. 'I told you,' she whispered. 'It's true—all of it!'

Suddenly, she looked vulnerable, dangerously vulnerable. He stared down into the pale blur of her face and saw the way she was biting her lip—no trace of the confident Kat Balfour now, he thought in surprise. 'What's true, Kat?' he questioned softly. 'Tell me what is frightening you so much.'

Kat trembled. It was the first time he had ever really spoken to her as an equal. The first time he'd shown her kindness, or consideration. It shouldn't have mattered but somehow it did—it mattered much more than it should have done. She tried telling herself that she shouldn't trust him—but somehow she couldn't help herself. Was it the protective warmth of his embrace which suddenly loosened her tongue—or the inexplicable understanding in his deep, accented voice which made her want to pour it all out?

'They killed him,' she whispered. 'They killed him and I couldn't stop them.'

'Who did?' he commanded urgently. 'Tell me, *Princesa*.'

'I don't know where to start,' she whispered.

'Start at the beginning,' he said simply.

And then words really started tumbling out—like feathers falling from a pillow which had been ripped wide open by a particularly sharp knife. Words she'd never spoken before. Words which her father had paid counsellors a small fortune to try to extricate from her and which instead she now found herself telling a cold-hearted Spaniard on a luxury yacht in the middle of the Mediterranean.

'I told you my parents didn't marry for love—but for c-convenience,' she stumbled. 'But then my mother met someone else— someone she knew could be special to her. My father felt it was only fair to let her go, and so they divorced, and she married Victor. He was a major in the army and he was lovely. Really lovely. And a good stepfather to me and my sisters.'

For a moment she allowed herself to re-member the happy times. Her mother being truly in love with a man for the first time in her life. The sense of being a proper family. The real bond which had existed between her and Victor. She had been the youngest girl and he'd spoiled her, treated her just like his own daughter. She remembered the joy of his promotion and the sense of excitement they all felt at the prospect of an exciting new country to live in. 'When he got posted to Sri Lanka, we all went with him,' she said slowly.

Carlos nodded and continued to stroke her hair, careful not to say anything in case he halted her flow.

'We were happy there. And then my mother had to take my sisters back to England, back to boarding school, the way she always did. And one night…' Her voice began to shake again. 'One night, while I was asleep… b-burglars b-broke into the house. There was nothing much to steal, but Victor challenged them. There was…there was a fight. I woke up and heard voices shouting, and then…then…'

This time he did prompt her even though he could feel the frozen fear in her body. 'Then?'

'I heard a gun go off!' she blurted out. 'I was so frightened that I just lay there. I was terrified that they were going to come up-stairs and shoot me.' For a moment she said nothing, her breathing shallow and rapid as she relived that night of violence.

'That's why you don't like fireworks,' said Carlos slowly, as he remembered her brief moment of fear in the boat.

Kat nodded.

'So what happened next?' he questioned softly.

She swallowed. 'I crept downstairs—to see the burglars fleeing. And that's when I found Victor. He'd been shot….' She swallowed, trying and failing to quell the pain of that awful memory. 'There was blood…*everywhere.*'

Carlos stilled. 'And?'

'He…he died.' She sucked in a shuddering breath. 'He died right there, in my arms.'

The hand which was at her back stilled, and instinctively he pulled her closer. Her hair brushed against him and he was fleetingly aware of its softness. 'He *died*?'

'Yes!' she sobbed.

'How old were you?'

'Ten.'

Ten. A child. An innocent, sheltered child. Beneath his breath, Carlos let free a flow of some of the more colourful curses he had learnt during his own chequered upbringing. He felt rage. More than rage—a sudden and unwanted sense of identification with her, because hadn't the trust of his own childhood been destroyed by the greed and violence of adults?

'A long time ago,' he said.

'Thirteen years.'

Was she really twenty-two? Hadn't he somehow thought that she was a couple of years younger than that? And hadn't it suited him to think that? To add her relative youth to the list of reasons why he shouldn't want her? But now that was forgotten as he found himself wanting to comfort her—she, a woman he had never imagined would need anything as basic as comfort.

'How often do you get this nightmare?' he demanded.

'Depends. When I hear fireworks. Sometimes a film can spark it off. Sometimes often, sometimes not.' She shrugged. 'It's random.'

Carlos nodded, and something about her listless body language made him want to reach out and take something of her pain away. 'You know, we're all products of our past, *Princesa*,' he said softly. 'And yours has been more tainted than most. But there are parts of it you have to let go. You have to, if you're going to live any kind of meaningful life.'

People had said it to her before, many times—but she had stubbornly refused to believe it. Yet when Carlos said it, the oddest sensation began to creep over her and Kat started to think that maybe he was right. That it *was* true. Was that because he'd never spoken anything to her but the stark truth, no matter how painful that could sometimes be? Or just because he seemed so confident and brash about life, so strong and powerful?

'I know I do,' she answered. 'It's just easier said than done.' She forced a note of lightness into her voice, wanting to dispel the heavy mood which seemed to have settled over them. She looked up at him. 'Any tips on how to go about it?'

He wished that the light scent she was wearing would not invade his senses with quite such unerring provocation. Or that her hair didn't feel like liquid silk spilling over his fingers. 'You have to tell yourself that you're more than a product of what happened to you,' he told her fiercely. 'Otherwise, it's like letting the perpetrators of the crime win.

Like allowing them to claim two victims, instead of only one. And you have to start believing that, as of now. Right now.' With the tip of one finger he tilted her chin upwards and looked deep into her eyes. 'Do you think you can do that?'

Kat thought how astonishing it was that he could quickly turn from sexy tyrant into a man of rare understanding—and yet didn't that make her want him even more? 'I'll try.'

'Good.'

But despite her tentative word of resolution, he could still feel the faint trembling of her body. Clearly, she was in some kind of reactive shock to the bad dream and had then relived it by telling him about it. And she was still locked in his embrace too. Carlos shifted slightly. It felt almost comfortable to have her leaning on him like that. A little too comfortable.

Suddenly, he let her go, pushing her back gently against the pillows, hardening his heart against the startled question in her eyes even as his body instinctively hardened to the soft promise in hers. 'Get back underneath the blankets,' he informed her tersely. 'You need to sleep.'

Sleep? It seemed as distant a possibility as dry land at that moment. And he had left behind an aching void. All Kat knew was that, without him, she felt cold and frightened again. Once more she bit her lip as a faint memory of the nightmare whispered over her skin and her eyes locked with his in terrified question. 'Where are you going?'

Where the hell did she think he was going? 'Back to bed.'

'Don't…' She swallowed, hardly daring to formulate the question, not wanting to open herself up to rejection once again. But Kat was not asking him to make love to her—she just wanted his presence to reassure her. To stay until the dream became a distant memory. 'Please don't go,' she whispered. 'Not yet. I'm…'

'What?'

'Scared.'

Carlos swallowed. Her slender limbs were splayed like a colt's and the ebony fall of her hair was spilling onto the pillow like dark satin. Reaching out, he clicked on the bedside lamp in the hope that extra light might dispel some of the unbearable intimacy of the setting. But it was a vain hope, because now she was bathed in a soft, apricot light which made her skin look completely edible.

How could he resist such a heartfelt plea— but what the hell was she asking of him? That he endure a temptation which was fast becoming unendurable? Staying close to the enticement of her body when his own was crying out to touch it?

Yet hadn't he always been the master of control in so many areas of his life before now? And surely this could be just another opportunity to prove his own inner strength and determination.

'Okay,' he bit out, and lay down beside her as gingerly as a man might lie beside a snake. 'I will stay, but only for a while. Understand?'

'Yes,' she whispered.

Instinct told him that it was pointless to leave her trembling on the other side of the big bed, and he intended the arm he reluctantly put round her shoulder to be nothing more than comforting as he pulled her close. A cuddle—even though, as a rule, he didn't do cuddling.

And he soon saw why. He had been a damn

fool to minimise the sensual impact of her slender body, despite the fact that it was covered with those rather prudish pyjamas. Or maybe that was what added to her allure. He'd never been to bed with a woman wearing pyjamas before. Come to think of it, he'd never been to bed with a woman and just lain there with a chaste arm around her shoulder either.

Kat snuggled against him, loving the way his fingers were now idly playing with her hair. Loving the solid reassurance of his powerful physique and the warmth of his nearness. 'That's nice,' she breathed.

He knew that. Too nice. Carlos didn't know how long he lay there for but it was long enough for his growing desire to stab like a heavy arrow at his groin. And if he didn't do something soon, she was going to pick up on it.

'Better?' he questioned thickly, wondering how soon he could make his escape, even while he silently mocked himself for his own hypocrisy. *Because you don't want to go anywhere, do you, Carlos?*

'Sort of,' she replied softly.

He rolled over, glad to be able to shift his position and to fractionally ease some of the terrible aching. 'Only sort of?'

'Well, like a big weight's been lifted, only I…' Suddenly, Kat felt awkward and wondered how she could ever have bared her soul like that. Especially to *him*—of all people. The man who was only tolerating her because he had to. Because he owed her father a favour. 'Listen, Carlos, maybe I shouldn't have unburdened myself—'

'Forget it,' he said curtly.

'It was crazy to have bottled it up for so long,' she said, half to herself. 'And in a funny sort of way, it feels so much better now that I've said it.'

In the soft glow of the apricot light, his eyes narrowed as he took in the full implication of her words. 'You mean you've never talked about it before? Not to anyone?'

'Never. I'm not really into counsellors— and it's not the greatest subject to bring up at parties, is it?'

'I can't believe that your father didn't tell me any of this himself,' he said, his voice growing bitter.

She stared at him. 'He didn't?'

'Of course he didn't! *Madre de Dios*, Kat! Do you really think I'd have brought you on board like this if I'd had any idea of the kind of trauma you'd suffered in the past?'

Actually, up until about half an hour ago, if someone had told her that Carlos Guerrero had a tiny pair of diabolical horns growing amidst the tumble of his dark curls, she would have believed them. But as she stared at his angry and shifting features, Kat realised that her feelings for him were undergoing a rapid change. Her physical attraction to him had never been in any doubt, but his surprising protectiveness towards her was forging an even more indelible mark than desire.

She shrugged, trying hard to focus on something else. To protect something of her family's reputation. And in so doing, surely to protect herself. 'Daddy's just a bit insensitive, that's all.'

'Please don't defend the indefensible!' And then something else occurred to him. 'Come to think of it, you must have known that I wouldn't have kept you here if I'd realised what had happened to you as a child. So why the hell didn't *you* tell me, Kat?'

Why indeed? She gave a brief smile. 'Because I can be stubborn,' she admitted. 'And proud'.

'*Sí*, I can imagine,' he commented drily, thinking how that tentative smile lit her face up. And how the apricot light of the lamp threw beguiling shadows over the pristine white of her top, emphasising the soft blue shadows which fell beneath the pert swell of her breasts.

'You know this changes everything?' he said suddenly.

She blinked up at him. 'What does?'

'After what you've told me, there's no way I can keep you on board. Not now.'

Kat stilled. She had rebelled against the lowly duties entrusted to her and being incarcerated on Carlos's luxury yacht, and she had wanted more than anything to escape. But while it was perfectly acceptable for *her* to object to staying, it was quite another for him to tell her she couldn't! She had always rebelled against authority, and she found herself protesting now. 'Why not?'

He wanted to say, *You know damned well why not.* But he didn't. Because once you openly acknowledged sexual attraction, it became almost impossible to resist. He wanted to tell her to stop looking at him as if butter wouldn't melt in those luscious lips of hers—because he knew that was simply an illusion. Yet their soft petal shape was putting him in danger, making him forget the conflict of interests raging within him.

'Because maybe you've learned a lesson after all,' he said. 'That you have to confront your demons in order to get rid of them, and that running away doesn't solve anything.'

Reality hit her with a harsh jerk. 'You're thinking about those rules,' she said slowly.

'*Sí.* The rules—and your father's wish that you learn the importance of commitment. I hope you have.' His voice hardened as he told himself that she was no longer his responsibility. 'But that is up to you, Kat. If you want to spend your life running away, then so be it, but I am no longer willing to be your enforcer. Not any more. I will order the crew to set sail for shore and as soon as we reach dry land in the morning—I can arrange to have you flown back to London.' His eyes narrowed in question. 'Unless there's somewhere else you'd prefer to go? France, maybe? Or perhaps the States?'

Kat swallowed. He was giving her back her liberty—but never had freedom seemed to mock her quite so much. She thought about how nomadic and pointless he made her life seem. The little rich girl with no real place to go—who could just choose where she wanted to flit around the globe, like someone idly stabbing a pin into a map.

She looked into those cold black eyes of his and suddenly a wave of longing washed over her—because didn't the cloak of darkness liberate her from convention? She didn't *want* to go and she didn't want to leave him—it was as simple as that. At least, not before she had sampled some of his magic. A taste of the sensual promise which radiated like an aura from his powerful frame, and which had ensnared her from the beginning.

She knew it was probably wrong and almost certainly foolish—because what if he pushed her away yet again? But Kat couldn't help herself. He had ignited a flame in her and she wanted Carlos Guerrero with a hunger she'd never experienced before. And maybe never would again.

She found herself wondering if a woman could just come out and tell a man that she wanted him. And wasn't it crazy that at the ripe old age of twenty-two, she didn't have a clue?

'Let's not talk about it now,' she whispered, and snuggled into the warmth of his bare torso.

Uncomfortably, Carlos shifted again—because now her appeal was growing by the minute, and acquiring all kinds of different dimensions on the way. Like a neglected kitten that had been brought inside and given food and shelter, she was looking up at him with something in her eyes which looked uncomfortably like trust.

He wanted to tell her not to trust him, that he never gave enough of himself to a woman to warrant such trust. But he knew from experience that even opening up a topic like that made women brighten. It made them think they were getting close to you. And there was only one way he wanted to get close to Kat Balfour…and no way was he going to give into it….

So why was his hand drifting down from her shoulder to her slender waist, the slick movement of his wrist bringing her soft body even closer? Like a drowning man he fought for control—a steely control and self-will which had always come as naturally to him as breathing. And to his fury and despair, he felt it slipping away from him.

'Kat…'

'Mmm?' All she was doing was whispering her lips against the line of his jaw and there wasn't anything so very wrong in that, was there? Not when he felt and smelt so warm and so *vital*.

'Kat.' Carlos swallowed, because the ability to speak coherently seemed suddenly to have deserted him. He felt his body tense with a sudden sense of urgency. 'If I don't get off this damn bed in a minute, I'm going to do something…something I'll regret.'

'Something like what?'

Just then she lifted her face to his, and the moment he felt her warm breath against his skin, Carlos knew that it was too late. 'Something like…this.'

Feeling the last of his self-control desert

him, he pulled her against his hard and hungry body. And with a small, angry curse, he began to plunder her lips with a hunger which now seemed unstoppable.

CHAPTER EIGHT

'OH!' KAT squirmed with pleasure as every fantasy she'd ever had about Carlos began to come true. She was in bed with the black-eyed Spaniard and he was kissing her—kissing her with the kind of passion she had somehow known existed, even if she'd never experienced it before. And somehow it didn't surprise her a bit to realise that she'd found it, with him.

'Oh!' Moaning softly, her body jerked in disbelieving reaction as he captured her breast, his fingers playing with one pert nipple which peaked against her cotton pyjama top. Sharp sensations of pleasure shot across its tightened bud and she could feel it begin to flower beneath his expert caress. Words slipped straight from her mouth and into his. 'Oh. That's...*gorgeous.*'

'You think I don't know that?' he growled.

Now the hand had slipped beneath the thin cotton top and made contact with the naked flesh there and she shuddered at that first intimate contact with her skin. 'C-Carlos!' she gasped.

'You want more?'

Breath drying in her throat, she nodded.

'How much more?'

'I—'

'This much?'

'Yes. Oh, yes.'

Trailing his hand down, he let it skate over the warmth of her belly and down beyond that to the faint fuzz of hair to where she was warmer still. Slicking his fingertips with soft precision to delve into her honeyed heat, he felt her buck beneath his touch.

'Carlos!' she gasped again.

Oh, but she was responsive—instantly and gratifyingly so—yet Carlos was a little taken aback by her unashamed hunger. Hadn't he expected her appetite to be jaded, as befitted a woman who must have enjoyed sex time and time and again? But instead she seemed almost *wondrous*...with a sense of near awe in her bright eyes as she cupped his face and kissed him back so passionately. Who would have thought it?

With the sleight of wrist which had made him so masterful in the ring, Carlos skimmed the little top up over her head and tossed it to the floor. Then he tugged at the matching bottoms, peeling them down over her hips before sliding them off completely. And, oh, she was beautiful—her body a creamy cascade of inviting curves and enticing shadows. '*Mía bella,*' he ground out unsteadily, as he caught hold of her fingers.

Her breath gasped against his neck as he guided her hand to the hard ridge at his groin, clearly discernable even through the thick denim of his jeans. 'C-Carlos,' she stumbled, her cheeks growing hot at this very physical evidence of how much he wanted her.

'I think I'm a little overdressed, don't you, *Princesa*?' he questioned unsteadily.

'Y-yes.' She should have been scared, but strangely enough fear was the last thing she was feeling as she heard the sound of his zip rasping down.

He moved away from her to remove the

jeans from his aching flesh—and then he was naked and so was she, and Carlos could never remember feeling so hard and hot and hungry before. Because this was forbidden? he wondered fleetingly as he stroked his finger-tips over her silken skin. He didn't know—and right then, he didn't care.

With one sure, swift movement, he moved on top of her and thought how light and how slender her body felt beneath his. 'Now,' he said huskily. 'Where shall I begin, *mía princesa*?'

'Anywhere,' she whispered, praying that he wouldn't expect her to take some sort of lead. To perform any kind of erotic act with him. The kind she'd heard her more experienced friends talk about. 'Anywhere you like.'

His mouth was at her throat as his hand moved down to the silken surface of her thighs, feeling them part beneath the soft insistence of his touch. He kissed her for an age, tempering his own hunger as he felt her melt into ever more willing compliancy. He touched her in places which made her moan, until he felt the restless urging of her body—and only then did he allow his own hunger to spiral up inside him. Technique and restraint were forgotten as he found himself compelled by a primitive urge to fill this woman, and for a moment he tensed, before driving into her body with what felt like the most powerful thrust of his life.

'Ah!'

A small sound was torn from her lips. A sound he'd never heard before. Feeling her flinch beneath that first exquisite thrust, Carlos lifted his head to see the briefest twist of discomfort cross her beautiful features. He stilled, his heart wrenching as he wrestled to take in the unbelievable implications of her reaction. 'Kat?' he questioned in disbelief.

Her eyes snapped open but she could read nothing in the dark, shuttered features, and suddenly Kat didn't want him to say the words out loud. Didn't want questions or explanations. Didn't want him to do anything but to carry on. The pain had passed now and she wanted it—she wanted *him*—just the way she'd always wanted him.

'Please,' she whispered, her voice slurred with the pleasure of feeling him inside her—

and a thought flew into her mind before she could stop it. *That this was what her body had been made for.* To have Carlos Guerrero's joined so intimately with hers. That this was exactly where she was supposed to be—and her heart turned over with longing. 'Make love to me.'

If Carlos hadn't been deep inside her, he might have objected to her choice of words—for what did this have to do with love? If her tight, virginal hotness hadn't been clamped around him in the most delicious way he could ever recall, he might even have had the strength to pull away from her.

But it was too late for that. Her innocence had been taken—unwittingly—by him. He couldn't undo what had already been done, so why not make the most of it?

His own hunger now put on hold, Carlos proceeded to employ every pleasurable technique he had ever learnt in the arms of a woman. And there were plenty of those. He knew that virgins notoriously had a disappointing introduction to sex and rarely orgasmed. Well, not this one. Oh, no. Miss Kat Balfour may have sprung on him the biggest surprise of all, but she would leave his bed knowing real pleasure.

He teased her and played with her. Withdrawing from her so that she gasped aloud with instinctive alarm that he wasn't going to continue. As if he would stop now! First tantalising her with the tip of his manhood as she gave breathless little moans of pleasure, he then drove deep inside her, so that the moans became gasps of pure joy.

He did it to her slow. Then fast. And just about every variation in between. And when he felt her pleasure begin to build to an unstoppable peak, he watched her. Felt her. Enjoyed the exquisite sensation as she spasmed around him. Saw her lips part and her back arch—and the corresponding rosy flush which bloomed all over her breasts. Heard the way she gasped his name.

Only then did he let go, allowing his own orgasm to wash over him with bittersweet waves which had never seemed quite so intense nor so long-lasting.

His body was still shuddering as he withdrew from her, taking a moment to steady his breath before turning to look at her, where

she was lying back against the bank of pillows, her body looking completely relaxed
and satiated but her eyes wary, and watchful.
But not nearly as wary as him.

Because Kat Balfour had just detonated his
image of her as a sexually experienced party
animal and blown it clean out of the water. It
had thrown him off balance—unsettled
him—and Carlos didn't *do* unsettled. After
sex he was used to turning over and going to
sleep—not lying there as feelings of disbelief
and anger began to build up inside him.
Propping himself up on one elbow, he sur-
veyed her flushed face and kiss-bruised lips.

'So,' he drawled. 'Am I supposed to be
flattered?'

There was an odd, fraught silence as his
question echoed round the cabin and Kat
found herself feeling lost, the dying waves of
her first-ever orgasm now muddied by the
mocking tone of his words. A sudden chill
iced her skin. His beautiful golden-olive
body was sprawled naked amid the rumpled
bedclothes and it should have felt perfect.
But the expression on his face drove home
the cold-blooded nature of his question,

leaving her wondering what she could possibly say in response. Because wouldn't a lie or an evasion only sound hollow?

Play it as cool as he is, she told herself, even though her heart felt as raw as her newly awoken senses.

'Flattered?' she answered softly. 'I don't know. You tell me.'

Black eyes iced into her. 'But that's precisely the point, isn't it? If there was any telling to be done, then it should have been you. Telling me.' He gave a short and disbelieving laugh, saying the words aloud in some vain hope that she might deny them. *That you'd never had sex with a man before.*

Kat swallowed. He made her virtue sound like a moral offence! But still she was determined to keep calm. She tried for her best light, cocktail-party tone. 'Is that how it's usually done, then—some kind of confession from the woman before it all begins?'

His face darkened. 'I wouldn't know, since you're the first virgin I've ever had.'

She tried to be flip. 'And did you like it?'

'Of course I liked it!' he bit out. 'It just might have been better if you'd warned me.'

Warned him? You *warned* people about ice on the road or about high winds at sea, but surely it was the wrong word to use when talking about the fact that a woman was completely innocent of men. Suddenly, faced by the censure which blazed from his eyes, Kat found the shaming words slipping from her lips, as if trying to offer him some kind of explanation. 'I thought…I thought it might spoil the mood.'

There was a pause. 'Damn right it would have done.' In fact, it would have spoilt the mood so completely that he would have dragged himself from her cabin—no matter how hot and how aching he'd been—and spent a night in bed alone with his frustration.

But instead… Instead, he had taken the sweet, curvaceous body she had offered him so willingly. Had entered her with a fierce hunger of his own and discovered that he was thrusting into hot virgin tightness. Carlos winced, for he was macho enough and old-fashioned enough to acknowledge virginity as sacred territory. And somehow he felt as if she'd *tricked* him into taking her. The protectiveness he had been feeling towards her after her nightmare had somehow been warped by what had just happened. As if she had cast some dark net over him and dragged him forcibly into her inner life—a place he had no desire to be.

And now… What the hell did he do now?

'*Madre de Dios*, I can scarcely believe it,' he exclaimed softly. 'You always look like you…'

Kat's heart missed a beat. 'Like I *what*, Carlos?'

He shrugged but didn't falter. 'Well, let's face it—you hardly dress or act like an innocent, do you?'

It hurt—and yet it was true, wasn't it? Apart from these past few days, she always dressed in haute couture—and sometimes those clothes were very provocative. Kat now saw that she might be guilty of sending out the wrong message entirely. And coupled with the way she'd come onto him at last year's Balfour Ball, who could blame him for thinking that she was a woman of the world, with many lovers in her past?

'Appearances can be deceptive,' she said quietly.

So could women, he thought bitterly. 'You should have told me.'

'And if I had?'

'I would never have done it, *Princesa*.'

'Maybe that's why I didn't.'

'So why?' His words were soft now. 'I mean, why me?'

She wanted to laugh. Was he *serious*? Possible explanations buzzed around in her head. She could tell him the truth. That he had enchanted her from the moment she'd laid eyes on him—and that on some subliminal level she'd always wanted him. Or would that inflate his already swollen ego? Fill him with fear that she might now demand some kind of commitment from him? Of course it would! Women always wanted Carlos—he had told her that himself—and she was no different from any of the others who had shared his bed. Just because she'd willingly given him her virginity wouldn't—and shouldn't—make a difference.

So she must show him. Show that she wasn't going to become needy or dependent. Wasn't going to fall in love with him. *She wasn't.*

Raking her hand back through her tousled hair, she shrugged, as if she'd given the question some thought. 'Well, you do have a bit of a *reputation*, Carlos.'

'Really?' he questioned silkily. 'Pray, enlighten me, *querida*. What kind of a reputation is that?'

'You're known in certain circles as a lover par excellence. And let's just say that I decided that it was time to lose my innocence.' Deliberately, she injected a nonchalant note into her voice. 'Virginity can become *such* a burden after a while. I wanted a lover and I wanted the best—and you, it seems, fitted the bill very nicely.'

He had never heard anything so outrageous in his life—and for a moment her sheer audacity took his breath away. But then the truth behind her words began to nag at him, like a rogue grain of sand which rubbed insistently at the skin. Because this was a scenario with which he was all too familiar. When he'd been a young matador, born on the wrong side of the tracks, rich and predatory women had made no secret of their desire to be possessed by his hard, powerful body.

And yet, hadn't she now made it easy for him? Easy for him to just give her one more taste of pleasure and then tell her that it wasn't going to happen again.

'Like a common stud, you mean?' he demanded hotly. 'A little bit of rough for the *princesa*?'

The accusation was angry and harsh, and completely at odds with what his hands were doing—for one was cupping her breast and feeling the nipple spring to instant life again beneath his questing fingers. While the other...

Kat gasped.

The other hand was inching its way down over her body once more and this felt like pleasure and punishment all in one. It was lingering provocatively on the swell of her belly and now it was skating down to the soft fuzz and the fork at her thighs—which instantly parted as if she were a puppet and he was jerking her strings. His fingers danced briefly on the warm cushions of her thighs and Kat held her breath...wanting him to touch her—not there, but *there*...where she ached so much that she began to squirm restlessly.

Waiting for an objection which never came, Carlos gave a low and savage laugh as a feather-light fingertip alighted with unerring precision at the hot, hard nub of her femininity. Felt her buck as pleasurable sensations rocketed through her.

'*Oh!*' she breathed.

'Oh, indeed.' Carlos groaned as he began to rub her sensitised flesh, watching her with almost clinical detachment as he brought her closer and closer to orgasm. He knew that she wanted him again—and he wanted it too—indeed he was hard enough to explode. But something stopped him from entering her body a second time. Something which niggled at the back of his mind and filled him with disquiet. But he carried on with what he was doing as he leaned to whisper in her ear.

'You know that this should never have happened?' he demanded. 'We're too different—we come from different worlds. Do you understand?'

'I...don't...*care*!' she gasped, greedy for him now. Wanting that amazing feeling to wash over her body once more and wanting the hard pressure of his kiss.

His finger still applying its remorseless rhythm, Carlos leaned over her and kissed her at the very moment of her orgasm. His lips quietened her soft squeal of delight and briefly he closed his eyes as she clung to him—her moment of vulnerable trust making him want to melt right into her. But he extricated himself from her arms as soon as it was decently possible. 'Go to sleep now,' he said roughly.

Pulling the sheet over the distraction of her naked body, he hardened his heart to the confusion in her blue eyes and the temptation of her embrace. More out of duty than passion, he lay down beside her, but he did not take her in his arms. Just lay there, listening to the sound of her breathing. At last, its rhythmical heaviness told him that she had drifted off, and his mind was able to focus on the unbelievable truth.

That for the first time in his life, he had neglected to protect himself while making love to a woman.

CHAPTER NINE

IN THE morning, of course, Carlos was gone. It came as no surprise to Kat to discover that there was nothing but an empty space beside her among the tangle of bedclothes. For hadn't he begun to distance himself from the moment he'd... She bit her lip and blushed with the memory. The moment his big body had shuddered inside hers and he had moaned something soft and fervent in his native tongue.

His very scent seemed to be in the air around her and it clung to her skin like a sensual perfume. Like a starving person who had enjoyed the most delicious meal, Kat found herself reliving every glorious moment in Carlos's arms. He had touched her *everywhere.* She found herself glancing down at her naked body, somehow expecting it to look different after what had happened. But it didn't. It just *felt* different. Or rather, she did. All soft and glowing and aching. Kat swallowed as she got out of bed and stared in the full-length mirror at the bright-eyed and tousled-haired woman who gazed back at her.

She had lost her virginity to Carlos Guerrero—and despite the fact that it had been a rapturous experience for her, on his part he had seemed *furious*. Maybe it was just a myth that men liked virgins, or maybe Carlos was just a rule to himself. But she still had to face him—and she would not crumple with any kind of shame in front of him. She would *not*.

Showering her newly sensitised skin, Kat dressed and went up on deck, though her heart was beating nervously as she walked out into the golden Mediterranean morning and prepared to face her lover.

But as she busied around fixing breakfast, she heard no sound to indicate that Carlos might be awake and ready to start work at the unearthly hour he always chose. In fact, he was nowhere to be seen—and for one awful moment Kat experienced a sensation of panic. What if…?

What if he'd simply gone off on his little motorboat like he had the other day? Left without saying goodbye, feeling unable or unwilling to face her in the cold light of day? Maybe regretting that the seduction had ever happened and trying to work out the most diplomatic way of extricating himself.

Kat cast her mind back to the previous night, remembering that after she'd told him all about her stepfather's death, he'd announced he intended to sail back to shore. And that he would no longer be keeping her on board, against her will. He'd told her, quite kindly, that he would send her on her way, without forcing her to work for him any more.

But that had been before he had taken her virginity, she reminded herself—before bringing herself up short. Because Carlos didn't *take* anything. She had *given* it to him—and what was more, she had given it to him eagerly.

And things had changed. She didn't feel as if she was on board *against her will*. She *wanted* to be here. But there was a reason for that, and Carlos was that reason.

She felt her stomach flip as he walked out on deck at that precise moment, carrying a file of papers in one hand and his laptop in the other. The dark glasses he wore hid his eyes but his face was as enigmatic as it always was. Her heart began to race erratically as her gaze ran over him, trying to conceal the hunger she felt, and the warm aching awareness she felt in his presence.

Was it normal for a woman to feel like this when she had just made love for the first time? she wondered. To experience strong feelings of emotional attachment towards the man who had shown you what real pleasure was? To feel all fluttery in his presence—and for your breath to catch in your throat, making breathing quite a feat?

'*Buenos días,*' he said, putting the papers and laptop down on the table. 'Did you sleep well?'

'I…well, yes,' she answered awkwardly, wondering what the protocol was—whether he would come over and take her in his arms and start to kiss her.

He didn't. He simply sat down at the table and began to pour a cup of the coffee she'd just made. 'Like some?' he questioned.

Kat swallowed down her disappointment, pride making her nod her head and force a smile as if the thought of a cup of coffee pleased her more than anything else. But inside she was hurting as the absence of a kiss or a hug told her as clearly as words that he regretted what had happened last night.

She took the cup he slid towards her. In a way, she might have preferred it if he was being angry—at least anger might have indicated that he felt *something* towards her. But this…this cool air of near impartiality was making her feel as if she had no substance at all. As if she hadn't gasped out her pleasure while his powerful body had filled her. And surely such cool indifference meant that he couldn't wait to be rid of her? So tell him you want to leave before you have the indignity of him asking you to go.

'So,' she said, careful to keep her voice steady. 'What time do you estimate we'll reach shore?'

Carlos's eyes narrowed—because this was not the reaction he had been anticipating. Women always clung to him like vines the day after he'd made love to them, pressing their bodies against him and urging him back between their soft thighs. Sometimes he succumbed and sometimes he didn't. But he *always* expected a come-on.

So why were Kat Balfour's bright blue eyes shuttered by the long sweep of her ebony lashes, and the lady herself doing a very good impersonation of an ice queen? And why was she talking to him in that cool and careful way, as if she was a completely different person from the one who had cried out her pleasure in his arms last night? Unexpectedly, he felt irritated.

'What are you talking about?' he questioned.

'You said that we would be sailing for shore today. You offered to fly me back to England—even America. Remember?'

'Yes, I remember,' he said slowly. 'But that was then. Things have changed now, Kat—you must realise that.'

Trying to keep the hope from her voice, Kat quickly put her cup down before she slopped hot coffee all over her lap. 'They have?'

'Of course.' For the first time, he recognised that the reality which had deprived him of sleep for much of the night had not even occurred to her. But then, why would it? This was a whole new territory for her. She was probably still getting used to the way her body felt and had given no thought to the potential bombshell it might now be concealing. He now had to think about the best way to put this. Only there *was* no best way, he realised. Just the bald, blunt truth. He stared at her. 'You do realise you could be pregnant?'

Kat's world stopped as the word spun. Round and round in her head it went. 'Pregnant?' she repeated blankly, as if it was something he had plucked at random from the dictionary.

Carlos's voice roughened. 'That *is* one of the consequences of having unprotected sex,' he said, and saw her mouth open in distress. 'Mea culpa, mea culpa!' he exclaimed bitterly, and slammed his fist on the table so that his cup half jumped out of its saucer. 'I blame myself! *I* was the experienced one. I was the one who should have used something. Who should not have been so overcome by lust that I failed to protect myself. Better still, I should have walked away.'

He was still trying to come to terms with

what he had done. That of all the people in the world, it should have been this blue-eyed heiress who had succeeded in making his legendary control dissolve. The kind of woman who epitomised everything he despised. And he had taken her virginity. Her purity lost on the bonfire of his lust. Contrition didn't come easily to a man who rarely considered himself to be in the wrong, but for once in his life Carlos recognised that contrition was due. 'For what it's worth, I'm sorry.'

'If it makes you feel any better, I feel exactly the same,' said Kat quickly, but inside her heart lurched with pain. Because this wasn't how it was supposed to be. She'd waited years and years to have sex—and every fairy-tale hope she'd attached to it was being systematically smashed by the Spaniard.

Oh, the physical expectations had easily been met—in fact, they'd surpassed her wildest dreams. It was this grim aftermath which was threatening to erode that ecstatic recall. She didn't want apologies and regrets that it had ever happened—she longed for him to take her into his arms and comfort her. And maybe kiss her too. Tell her that he adored her, leaving her free to admit that he was already occupying a sizeable place in her heart, despite all her determination not to let him.

Well, it's your own stupid fault, tormented the voice of her conscience which she had been failing to quieten all morning. *It was you who was hell-bent on having this man to be your lover. And he made it clear that you were the kind of woman he despised, so you have only yourself to blame for the consequences.*

Carlos looked at her, thinking how pale and pinched her face looked this morning. And suddenly, his imagination conjured up an image of his seed—one of the many seeds he had planted in her last night—growing into a baby. A *baby.* Beside his coffee cup, one hand balled into a tight fist as a strange, nameless emotion caught in his throat. 'Our feelings on the subject are irrelevant,' he said unevenly. 'What we have to decide is what to do next.'

'Well, I want to get off this boat as soon as possible,' she put in, determined to beat her own retreat before she was evicted. 'Just the way we'd planned.'

Carlos narrowed his eyes. *You and me both, Princesa*, he thought. And not just because the idea of her working on his yacht now seemed intolerable after everything that had happened. Last night had been a spur of the moment thing—a gesture of comfort which had escalated into something else. Being cooped up on board with her—having once tasted the pleasure of her delicious body—would stretch his resolve to breaking point. *But it wasn't going to happen. Not again. It wouldn't be fair. Certainly not to her.* And in the meantime…

'When will you know?' he demanded.

She stared at him blankly. 'Know?'

His black eyes were fixed on her face. Didn't her rich-girl's education provide basic classes in biology? he wondered bitterly. 'Whether or not you're carrying my child.'

Colour flooded into Kat's cheeks, because this question seemed almost as intimate as what they had done together last night. And bizarrely, the thought of a tiny, black-haired baby with golden-olive skin—a miniature Carlos—did not fill her with the dread and fear she would have expected. Instead, she felt an unbearable sense of longing wash over her and she shook her head in slight disbelief.

How crazy was that? Letting her mind do a few swift calculations, she stared at him. 'In about two weeks.'

Carlos didn't react, and neither did he point out the obvious. That they had chosen her most fertile time to make love. 'In that case, I think you should stay here, with me,' he stated flatly.

Kat stared at him, trying desperately to keep the naked hope from her eyes. 'Why?'

He took off his shades then and, for the first time, Kat noticed the dark shadows beneath his ebony eyes and the undeniable strain around his sensual lips. As if he hadn't slept a wink.

'Where else are you going to go?' he questioned.

Had he intended to make her sound like some piece of unwanted luggage which had turned up on his doorstep? Twisting her fingers in her lap, Kat thought about her options. 'My family own a couple of apartments in central London. Or there's always…home…'

But as she thought of her mother's gatehouse or of the magnificent Balfour Manor itself, her voice trailed off unconvincingly. Was that because *nowhere* ever really felt like home and never had, except for that halcyon period in Sri Lanka, before Victor died? She'd never experienced that real sense of *belonging* which other people seemed to take for granted. Of knowing her place in the world, and where she fitted in. But if sleeping with Carlos had succeeded in making her feel even more alienated, she was certainly not going to let *him* know that. Kat lifted a defiant chin. 'I can always go there.'

'No, you can't go there,' he contradicted firmly. He had noticed the unmistakable tremble of vulnerability on her lips—and it suddenly occurred to him that maybe Kat Balfour was not the woman he had thought her to be. 'Not with this preying on your mind. People will notice that you are pale and distracted and they will want to know why.'

'And of course I won't be able to tell them, will I?' she demanded hotly. 'Because that might just compromise the mighty Carlos Guerrero's integrity!'

He flinched, unable to deny her angry accusation. 'It might just create a whole host of unwanted problems for you as well, *Princesa*,' he answered quietly. 'Particularly if it isn't true.'

'And if it *is* true?' she questioned, her voice rising a little. 'What, then? Won't that pose even more problems?'

There was a long pause as he tried to imagine Kat Balfour giving birth to his baby, and when he spoke his voice sounded empty. 'Of course it will, but nothing that can't be worked out. And in the meantime…'

Hesitation was not something she associated with him, and Kat looked at him with a sudden nervous trepidation. 'What?'

Black eyes regarded her and Kat thought how suddenly *cold* they had become.

'I think it would be better for both of us if we viewed what happened last night as a one-off,' he said softly.

Suddenly, despite the blazing heat of the Mediterranean sun, she found herself shivering. Better for *both of us*, he had said—but that was surely a lie. It was better for *him*, that was all. He was obviously the kind of man who could swat away memories of a woman once he'd bedded her. Whereas she…why, she was in terrible danger of concocting fantasies about her Spanish lover, if she wasn't careful. But somehow she nodded, even managed to conjure up a faint smile. Sometimes she had seen her sense of pride as a burden, but now she saw it as her saviour.

'Much better,' she agreed calmly. Two weeks of waiting and wondering if there was a baby on the way—and all the while she and Carlos would be like polite strangers. Could she go through with it? Or would the effort of maintaining such a pretence drive her mad?

Yet the alternative was far more daunting. Stuck in Balfour Manor or one of the London apartments with such a massive secret eating away at her.

'Why not just regard the next couple of weeks as a kind of holiday while you wait to find out?' he continued coolly. 'The kind of holiday you first envisaged when you were brought here. You can lie around on deck, doing nothing more taxing than sunning yourself by the pool, and reading magazines. I'm sure you can find enough to amuse you.'

The words hung in the air and mocked her. He made her sound like some spoilt little girl who needed to be entertained. But that was how he saw her, wasn't it—even now? How he'd always seen her. Some vacuous little airhead.

Well, damn Carlos Guerrero. She would go crazy if she had to mooch around on deck acting as if there wasn't this great time bomb waiting to go off.

'I don't want to lie by the pool reading magazines, Carlos,' she said slowly.

His eyes narrowed with surprise as he stared at her. 'You don't?'

'No. I'd like to carry on cooking for the crew. That *is* what I'm supposed to be here for.'

'Are you serious?'

'Entirely serious. I was just starting to get into it—and there are plenty more things left for me to learn. So if you'll excuse me, I'd better get on with the preparations for today's meals.' The decision which had clearly surprised him now empowered her enough to give him a serene smile. 'Don't worry. I'll let you know when lunch is ready.'

Carlos stared at her, his eyes narrowing with frustration. What the hell was the matter with her? She hadn't flirted or pouted—and now she was proposing to carry on working!

He felt the sudden leap of desire as she picked up her coffee cup, and he lifted his hand in a silent gesture of command, dampening down the voice of reason which was demanding to be heard.

'I want you eating your lunch up here with me today,' he informed her silkily. 'Understand?'

Kat stared into the shuttered black eyes, convinced that his autocratic statement had more to do with possession than because he actually enjoyed her company. Wasn't it just a demonstration of his power over her—and could she possibly maintain this air of nonchalance if she had long periods of being alone with him?

'As you wish,' she said carelessly. 'You're the boss after all.' And she headed off towards the galley.

Carlos was left looking at the empty space she left behind with a feeling of disbelief, and it was several minutes before he was able to lose himself in his work.

But he wasn't deaf to the sounds of laughter which occasionally drifted upwards from the galley, and as the morning wore on, he found that his mood was growing increasingly sour. So that by the time Kat appeared, bearing a bowl of salad and some sort of pasta dish, his nerves were frayed and he felt the slow and relentless beat of frustration.

'Hungry?' she questioned with a smile which sent his pulse rate soaring.

'I can always eat, *Princesa.*'

Sitting down opposite him, Kat wondered if he knew that her heart was racing erratically or that the desire to touch him felt almost like a physical *pain*. What on earth were they going to talk about, when all she could think of was how it felt to have his warm skin next to hers. Especially when he was behaving as if she was completely invisible. *Pretend you're at some tedious social function and have just been sat next to the guest of honour.*

'Why don't you tell me how you got into bullfighting in the first place?' she enquired politely, doling out a spoonful of pasta onto one of the plates.

There was a pause. 'I thought I told you I don't like talking about it?' he snapped.

'Did you? Okay. Then let's try something else.' She picked up a dish of salad and held it towards him with a polite smile. 'Tell me about your business interests instead, Carlos. How you got started, how you made the jump from bullfighter to international tycoon—that must be quite some story.'

Black eyes were narrowed at her in disbelief. She sounded like one of those women he occasionally ran into at diplomatic parties— the kind who had been schooled in making polite small talk to a variety of guests. And Kat would have grown up learning how to do that too, he recognised. 'I don't want to talk about my damned business either.'

She shrugged. 'Well, we've got to talk about *something* over the next couple of weeks, haven't we? Otherwise what else are we going to do?'

Carlos stared at the blue-black gleam of her ebony hair and felt all his good intentions dissolving by the second. Her blue-eyed beauty and breezy attitude were shattering his equilibrium and making a mockery of his determination not to touch her—but when he stopped to think about it, why had he insisted on her joining him for lunch unless it was to do precisely that?

'Put the dish down, Kat,' he said slowly.

'What did you think I was going to…?' But her bravado suddenly deserted her as she saw something written on his face—a look which pierced her heart and her body like an erotic arrow. It was desire—raw, undisguised and urgent. 'C-Carlos?' she questioned, her voice and her hand shaking as she put the pasta down. 'What do you think you're doing?'

'I'll give you three guesses.'

He was on his feet now, moving with the lithe grace of some dark panther as he stalked towards her, as if he were the predator and she his prey. Almost roughly, he pulled her into his arms and Kat stared up at him in confusion.

'But you said…' she whispered in confusion.

'To hell with what I said—I've already broken every rule in the book for you, Kat Balfour, so why not break one more and have done with it?' he demanded, as his mouth came down hungrily on hers.

The kiss was hot, breathless. Two mouths meeting and mingling with urgent greed. Kat

shuddered as her hands flew to his shoulders
while his own snaked possessively around
her waist. She tried telling herself that his
stark declaration of desire hadn't contained
a single word of affection, and surely she
shouldn't settle for that. But as his lips continued to sweetly plunder hers, all her doubts
just melted away. Sucked into the powerful
vortex of newly awoken desire, she found
herself wondering just where all this was
going to lead. Up here, on deck…surely he
wasn't planning to…to…

But abruptly, he terminated the kiss and,
catching hold of her hand, wordlessly led her
towards his cabin.

Kat hadn't been in Carlos's bedroom since
she'd taken that rather resentful tour of the
yacht on the day she'd arrived, before he had
flown in by helicopter. It seemed a lifetime
ago, and yet she could count off the days on
one hand. A few days and your life could
change for ever….

'Carlos—'

'Do you know what we're going to do for
the next two weeks?' he questioned silkily. 'I
am going to take you to heaven and back,

Princesa. I am going to show you a hundred different ways to make love.' His voice dipped. 'And then a hundred more.'

'I...I—'

'Sssh. Just kiss me,' he commanded unsteadily.

An unmistakable note of hunger had now deepened his voice and it was strong enough to make her forget her fears. Strong enough to make her feel his equal again—her, the woefully inexperienced Kat Balfour feeling the equal of this worldly wise and powerful Spaniard. How crazy was that? But she did. In that hot and breathless moment she *did*. 'Oh, Carlos,' she whispered helplessly, as she drifted her mouth against his.

Inexplicably, Carlos's hands were trembling, and for the first time in his life he had difficulty yanking down the zip on a pair of woman's jeans. But Kat proved bold. She slid his silk shirt off as if she had just been taught the most erotic way to remove an article of clothing—and where she laid his flesh bare, her lips followed, anointing tiny butterfly kisses on his skin.

Her soft, sweet seduction almost took his

breath away, and Carlos tumbled her down onto the silken counterpane which covered his vast bed, his hands reacquainting themselves with all her soft curves and secret places as if it had been months since he'd last touched her body, instead of hours. Burying his head between the lush warm globes of her breasts, he could feel her squirm with excitement beneath the flickering path of his tongue. His mouth drifted to one rose-peaked nipple and he heard her gasp as it puckered in his mouth.

'Carlos!'

'*Sí, Princesa—qué pasa?*'

Kat's fingers tangled in his black curls as waves of pure pleasure washed over her. 'K-kiss me.'

'Oh, I will kiss you,' he murmured, with a low growling laugh. 'Don't you worry your beautiful head about that.'

Kat had meant a kiss—a *proper* kiss—but now his dark head was drifting down towards her belly. And his tongue was sliding into the faint dip there and flicking at her so playfully that she felt quite faint. He was certainly kissing her, but…kissing her *there*? She shuddered as a wave of pleasure racked through her body, accompanied by another wave of disbelief and wonderment. 'C-Carlos.'

'Mmm?' Now his lips were brushing over the soft fuzz of hair between her thighs, hearing her tiny gasp as he parted her legs and began to lick at her honeyed sweetness.

Kat couldn't talk. Couldn't think. She was aware that she was trembling as tiny shimmerings of pure excitement began to build inside her, promising the same pleasure as he'd bestowed on her during the night. Just as she was aware of the sensation of Carlos's mouth kissing her at the focal point of her femininity. It felt almost unbearably intimate and yet—bizarrely—it also felt like the most natural thing in the world.

The shimmerings now became little peaks—a whole range of sensations which began to hum and throb deep inside her, like a heavily laden honeybee about to topple from a flower.

'Oh!' she breathed—and then she clutched his broad shoulders. 'Oh, oh, *oh*!'

Inhaling the distinctive scent of her arousal, Carlos sucked deeply on her throbbing flesh while she orgasmed against his mouth, her sighs of satisfaction sounding like tiny gasps of disbelief.

He moved back up to lie over her, brushing her tousled black hair away from her flushed face. 'You liked that?' he asked eventually, a finger moving to trace the trembling outline of her lips.

Liked it? Kat was so overawed by what had just happened to her—so seduced by the subsequent gentling of his tone—that she couldn't hold back on the way she was feeling. Lifting her hand to one olive cheek, she let it trail deliciously over the dark rasp of his jaw. 'It was…it was wonderful.'

'Then let's make it even more wonderful, shall we?' But this time he reached for the condom he'd laid in readiness by the bedside and he saw her watching him from between slitted blue eyes as he carefully ripped open the wrapping. 'Better not make the same mistake again,' he declared, as he took her into his arms once more, softening her with kiss after kiss until she was ready for that first sweet thrust.

And afterwards, Kat lay there, curled

against his hard body, watching the sunlight which was shafting in from the portholes while one word danced around in her mind. *Mistake,* he had said, as he had slid on the protection and moved over her with dark intent in his eyes.

Carefully, she turned her head to look at him, but his eyes were closed—the harsh lines of strain on his face now dissolved by the recuperative power of sleep. In repose, his face seemed softer, but no less formidable for that. The strong line of his jaw and the proud slash of his cheekbones still spoke of a certain arrogance, and strength.

His was the face and the body of the hunter—strong and powerful—with the finest genes and an unmistakable air of dominance. The kind of man that nature had conditioned women to desire. Instinctively, Kat let her hand flutter down to lie on her belly. How flat it felt—and yet, even now, his child might be growing there. Layer upon layer of tiny cells building by the minute, the hour. How big would it be by the end of the week? By the end of two?

Her heart gave a leap of something which

felt uncomfortably close to excitement and, with an effort, she forced the thought away. But then, she'd had a lot of practice at pushing away disturbing memories. And it was pointless getting worked up by a pregnancy which probably didn't exist outside her imagination.

What if it did? What if she was carrying the Spaniard's child?

How had Carlos described it? Kat bit her lip, remembering the sudden tightening of his hard features and the words he had used.

Carlos had not viewed the prospect with anything other than a dark foreboding— hadn't he made that clear with the very word he'd used?

A *mistake*, he had said.

CHAPTER TEN

'So how exactly *did* you get into bullfighting?'

Carlos slid the cork from the bottle of wine and slanted her a look of irritation as he poured some into her glass. '*Infierno*, Kat— why won't you give up on that?'

'Because I'm curious, that's all. You know pretty much everything there is to know about me, Carlos, but you always get so tight-lipped about your own past.'

Staring at him across the table, which tonight—like most nights—she'd laid on deck beneath the stars, Kat didn't bother pointing out that they had to talk about *something*. They couldn't spend every spare minute having glorious sex and revelling in its lazy aftermath, as the luxury yacht skimmed the sapphire waters of the Mediterranean and they waited to find out if she was having his baby. It was the elephant in the room. The subject they never touched on.

Yet it was funny how life sometimes adapted to the strangest situations. Or maybe that was the enduring wonder of the human spirit—that you always got on and made the best of things. And with Carlos conducting business deals and Kat cooking up increasingly ambitious meals, sometimes it felt like playing house. Even if deep down she knew that all they were doing was a form of displacement therapy, while they tried to ignore the great question mark which hovered over them.

Sometimes it frightened her—the ease with which she had been able to push the burning issue far from her mind and to concentrate instead on the proud, dark allure of her Spanish lover. Even if she knew that she was storing up danger for the future—because she had started to care for him in a way which would never be reciprocated.

She had become his eager and responsive lover—though time after time she had told herself it was crazy to become emotionally involved with a man whose heart was famously as cold as ice. Why, hadn't he warned her of that himself when he'd recounted with amusement just why his yacht had been given its unusual name of *Corazón Frío*? A Spanish newspaper had nicknamed him 'Cold Heart' because of a particularly ruthless takeover bid he had executed—which had coincided with a starlet selling her story of their doomed relationship. And Carlos had shown complete contempt for the article by adopting the name for his superyacht.

As the days ticked by, Kat found herself in a terrible dilemma—knowing that she should be praying that there *was* no baby. Because Carlos didn't want a baby—he had made that quite clear.

'If you are pregnant, then we will cope,' he had stated in a flat voice which she had found especially chilling. 'And our child will never want for anything.'

Except two parents who loved each other, Kat realised miserably.

Her troubled thoughts cleared and Kat found Carlos staring at her across the table, his expression curious as he pushed away his plate.

'You were miles away, *Princesa*,' he observed softly.

Grateful for the candle-light which disguised a multitude of emotions, Kat shrugged. 'Well, there's a lot to think about.'

'And it makes you frown?' he prompted.

'Sometimes.' She met the question in his eyes. 'Well, it's not exactly...ideal—this situation we find ourselves in,' she said carefully. 'Is it?'

There was a pause and Carlos gave a ragged sigh, knowing that evasion would be kinder. But ultimately, what could he say—other than the truth? 'No, of course it isn't. But there's no point in discussing it until we know one way or the other, is there? I thought we'd already decided that.'

'Which is why I was asking you about bullfighting.' Kat's voice lowered defensively. 'I'm certainly not trying to invade your precious privacy, Carlos—just trying to make conversation.'

His eyes narrowed as he looked at her. Was he really the tyrant she sometimes hinted at? And if she was expecting his child, then did she not have the right to know something of his past?

But where to begin? He stared at her across the flickering candle-light. 'We were poor,' he said simply. 'And I mean dirt poor. My mother used to work around the clock to provide for us—in fact, I hardly saw her when I was growing up.'

Kat remembered some of the remarks he'd made about spoilt, wealthy women. Was that why he had sounded so caustic—because his own mother had had nothing? 'And…your father? What about him?'

'My father?' He gave a short laugh. 'Oh, my father was too busy chasing his dreams of being Spain's best matador to care about anything or anyone.'

'So he was a bullfighter too?'

He drank a little more wine. 'He was, until a horrific accident in the ring led to the loss of his arm—and the even greater loss of his dreams. For a while he was a broken man, until he realised that he might be able to live out those ambitions through his son. And that is what he set about doing.'

There was an odd, brooding kind of silence. 'So?' she prompted softly.

His mouth twisted. 'So he sat me on my first bull at three.'

'Three?' Kat echoed in horror.

'At five he armed me with my first sword,' continued Carlos implacably. 'And because Spanish law decrees that novice bullfighters must be at least sixteen, at ten he uprooted us all to Central America—where the rules are more...*relaxed.'*

He shrugged and there was another odd kind of silence while Kat watched a series of conflicting emotions chasing across the hard, handsome face of her Spanish lover. 'And did you like it?' she whispered. 'Bull-fighting, I mean.'

'I loved it,' he said unexpectedly. 'And I was good at it.' There was a pause, before he gave a brief, hard smile. 'Too good.'

'How can you be too good at something?'

'Because it makes it difficult to walk away, even when you know it's the right thing to do. I left the ring when I was barely twenty—when I was on the brink of a glittering career.' His voice lowered as his mind took him back to that hot and dusty day—remembering the heat and the dust, the strong smell of death. 'I made the kill, dropped my cloak and, as the crowd grew silent, walked away without a backward glance.'

There was a moment as Kat registered the sheer drama of his words. 'But why?' she whispered.

Carlos looked at her, knowing that, like her, he had secrets which at times had proved unbearable—and like her, he had buried them deep. How could a man admit to the humiliation of having been forced to endure cruelty in his own home? The fierce beatings he had suffered at the hands of his father. Because hadn't that cruelty made him the man he was today?

'Because my father beat me,' he said slowly. 'In fact, he spent most of my childhood beating me. It was all about control. To show me who was boss. To get me to do what *he* wanted—which was to be the greatest bullfighter in the world. And then, when I was a teenager and old enough to stand up for myself, he stopped.' He paused, and his eyes glittered. 'Because by then there was no longer any need to threaten me with physical violence since I stood on the brink of a career he had coveted all his life. Success and riches and fame were all there for the taking.'

Kat stared at him. 'And that's why you walked away from it,' she breathed. 'You took back control of your life—and, in doing so, you were punishing him for all the hardships you'd endured at his hands.'

Carlos nodded, her perception surprising him, even though he found it slightly unnerving. 'Exactly.'

Kat nodded. It made more sense now—or rather, *he* did. He had known brutality and hardship on a scale which few others would identify with—and not only because he had been beaten by his father. Fancy putting a little boy of three on a bull and then two years later presenting him with a real sword. No wonder they called him Cold Heart!

She rose to her feet. The expression on his face expressly told her that he did not want any sympathy. In fact, there was only one thing which she was in a position to give him—and maybe not for much longer. *Because if she wasn't pregnant, what then?* She tried to push the unwelcome thoughts from her mind—but one in particular kept coming back to taunt her. *That if he hadn't taken her virginity, then he would have put her on a plane back to London days ago and it would all be over. She was only here because she had to be.*

But still she went over to him and put her arms around his neck, tenderly nuzzling her lips in the thick dark curls which grew around its nape. And, as if sensing her thoughts, he lifted his head to look at her, but his eyes were shuttered.

'Any day now, you should know?'

'Yes.' The question took her by surprise and she found herself resenting it for all kinds of reasons. It made her feel like some hen sitting on top of an egg, waiting to see if it was going to hatch. Suddenly, she saw the vivid image of her body as a cage, its contents having the potential to trap them both with a baby they'd never planned. And Kat shuddered—for how on earth could she bear to trap a man like Carlos, a man who had spent his childhood trapped by his father's ambition?

In the muted light of stars and candles, Carlos observed her tense reaction to his question and narrowed his eyes. 'You don't want to be pregnant, do you?' he bit out harshly.

She walked away from him, distractedly shaking her head to halt words which seemed intrusive—afraid that she might give herself away, because how could she possibly explain to him all her mixed emotions? Especially when he'd never made any secret of the fact that he didn't want a baby. He hadn't even wanted an affair with her, had he? *We are too different,* he'd said.

But Kat knew that she couldn't dwell on Carlos's lack of feelings for her. She had to be strong. She would cope with whatever hand fate had dealt her. And if she *was* pregnant, then she would love his baby with a fierce love, but she would not hold Carlos Guerrero ransom to fate. It would not be fair, not after all that he had told her. She shook her head. 'Not now, Carlos,' she whispered. 'I don't want to discuss it. In fact, I'm…I'm tired. I'm going to bed.'

His mouth hardened—angry with himself for having broken a lifetime rule of non-disclosure. Why the hell had he poured out all that poison about his childhood? And angry too at the way his rashness—his *lust*—had the potential to complicate Kat Balfour's life in a way she'd never envisaged. Nor deserved. 'So go,' he said abruptly. 'I'm not stopping you.'

She did—but for once he didn't follow her, though she waited and waited with breathless expectation, until she realised that her wait was in vain. Eventually, she must have fallen asleep because when she awoke in the cold, grey hours of dawn, Carlos was not beside her—and a chill feeling of dread stole over her heart. Creeping from her cabin, she went to look for him, half hoping he might still be out on deck, perhaps having fallen asleep where he sat.

But the deck was empty and, for once, the light there was gloomy, the stars fading into insignificance in the pearly light and the first blush of sunrise not yet visible. In the distance she could see the faint twinkling of lights and Kat blinked her eyes in surprise. Land. Funny how it could just loom up and surprise you—when all you'd seen for days were just different variations of a stunning sea. Yet, all the time, the yacht was moving—

taking them back towards France from where they'd started. And Kat realised that Carlos had cleverly timed it to coincide with her finding out whether or not she was pregnant.

Barefooted, she tiptoed to his cabin, and when the door swung quietly open it was to see his sleeping form sprawled on the bed. He had flung the bedclothes away and was lying there—gloriously naked—outlined like a golden statue against the pristine whiteness of the sheet.

His black hair was ruffled and she found herself gazing lovingly at his face—the proud lips and the haughty slash of cheekbones. She remembered what he had told her about his heartbreaking childhood—about his cruel father and a mother who sounded weak and put-upon. Was that why she had not been able to put a stop to her son's beatings? she wondered sadly—and Kat's heart turned over with a love she knew he was not seeking.

As she stood there silently watching him, his dark eyes fluttered open.

'Kat?' But he said it with all the emotion of someone saying *window* or *door*, and for a moment, their gazes locked—until she realised that he seemed to be gazing right through her. As if he hadn't really seen her. Or hadn't really wanted to. And then he turned over and went right back to sleep.

A dull kind of pain cloaked her heart as she crept back to her own cabin—but during the night came a different and very familiar kind of pain. Snapping on the bedside light, she found herself staring down at the crimson flowering of blood with eyes which were inexplicably filled with tears.

And it was a white-faced and trembling Kat who was already dressed and on deck the following morning when Carlos emerged.

'You're up early,' he observed.

'You didn't come to bed last night,' she accused, wondering if she was hiding the trembling hurt in her voice.

Dark eyebrows rose in arrogant query. 'Are you nagging me, Kat?'

'I'm just asking a question.'

He remembered the way she had shuddered when the subject of pregnancy had come up. Her avowal that she had no desire to have a baby. And even though her words made complete sense, something in her statement had filled him with distaste. So that he had been glad to spend the night apart from her—yes, *glad*. For what man would want to make love to a woman when she'd just told him something like that? 'You said you were tired,' he said coldly.

Was that the only reason? Kat wondered—as she registered the sudden iciness in his voice. Or was he regretting everything he'd told her about his tortured childhood? Had he wanted to distance himself after the confidences he'd shared—or simply decided that the affair had now run its course?

Well, in that case, his wish was about to come true. Biting her lip, she looked up into his hard and handsome face, trying to tell herself that this was all for the best, even if it felt as if her heart was breaking in two. 'Well, anyway—all that's irrelevant now. I've…well, it's good news really,' she said.

'Oh?'

'I think…' She swallowed down the terrible feeling of loss which had washed over her and presented him with a resolute face instead. 'I'd like someone take me ashore please, Carlos.' She met the cool

question in his eyes but she didn't flinch,
even though the unbearable intimacy of what
she was about to say made her cheeks turn
hot. 'That is unless you happen to carry
sanitary protection on board.'

CHAPTER ELEVEN

AN ATMOSPHERE like a heavy blanket greeted her announcement and Kat insisted on being ferried ashore as quickly as possible. She just wanted to get away from the yacht—and away from the cool indifference with which Carlos had greeted the news that there wasn't going to be a baby.

'I'll take you,' he told her, as she appeared back on deck after packing her bags, her face set and her mouth composed in a thin line.

But Kat shook her head. And have her breaking down and making a complete fool of herself in front of all the jet set milling around the port at Antibes? Risk telling him how empty her life was going to feel without him—or even worse, beg him to let her stay?

'No,' she said, and wobbled him an attempt

at a smile. She wasn't going to cry. She *wasn't*. 'It's better this way, Carlos. We're both relieved at the outcome, you know we are.' So why did her heart feel as if someone had taken a dagger to it and driven a gaping great wound into its centre?

'*Sí*,' he said slowly. 'You are right. It is better this way.'

Her voice was determinedly bright. 'Well, then, there's nothing more to be said, is there?'

He let his eyes drift over her, taking in the soft skin and the beautiful lips—and the eyes which were as blue as a Mediterranean sky. 'Except that it was a pretty amazing affair while it lasted,' he observed softly.

'Yes. Yes, it was.' Was this what he usually said—his farewell line? A whole script prepared to ease the pain of the parting, cleverly couched to sound almost *tender*, but cautious enough not to whip up any false hope. And suddenly Kat knew she couldn't face anything which masqueraded as tenderness, because that would just make this parting even more unbearable. Her fingers clenching into a fist over the handle of her bag, she stared up at him. 'But it's over now.'

Carlos had never been left quite so swiftly nor so efficiently by a woman before. Come to think of it, it was always him that did the leaving. Hadn't he wondered whether Kat might try and drag it out a bit longer, digging in her delectable heels and intimating that she had no desire for their affair to end? Well, she hadn't—and once again she had confounded all his expectations. His eyes narrowed. And maybe she was right. Maybe it really *was* better this way.

Leaning over, he planted the briefest of kisses on her trembling lips just as Mike appeared from the galley.

'Look after her,' said Carlos abruptly, and turned and walked away.

Kat's heart sank as she watched his retreating back, but what had she expected? That he might stand there watching her wave a dinky little hanky as the speedboat put more and more distance between them? Why, he was probably heaving a huge sigh of relief—like a man who had just been relieved of a mighty burden.

She felt slightly ill as she stepped ashore, where Carlos had a car waiting for her, and was startled by a sudden blue flash.

'I think somebody just took my photo,' she said in confusion.

'Oh, there's always paparazzi hanging around here,' said Mike with a shrug, as he hauled out her bags and put them on the quayside. And then, to her surprise, he enveloped her in a brief bear hug. 'We're going to miss you,' he said gruffly. 'You've done good.'

The farewell only added to her highly emotional state and, once Mike had gone, she clambered into the back of the car, directing it to stop at a *pharmacie*. And afterwards she was whisked to a nearby airstrip, where Carlos had arranged for a jet to fly her to London.

As soon as she'd touched down, her cellphone started ringing, with her father on the other end of the line.

'Kat,' he said gruffly. 'Are you okay?'

'I'm…fine,' she answered warily. 'Why?'

'I've just had Carlos Guerrero on the phone.'

For a moment she froze as the Spaniard's dark and golden features danced provocatively in her mind. 'What…what did he say?'

'Just that he was very pleased with you.'

'He…he did?'

'He certainly did. Said that you seemed to

have been cured of your tendency to run away from problems, that you seemed to have learned the meaning of the word *commitment*, and that I should be very pleased with you. Oh, and he also advised me to let you have use of the London flat and start paying your allowance again.'

The breath which she only just realised she had been holding escaped from Kat's lips with a sigh. But really, what had she expected? That Carlos would tell her father that he'd become incredibly close to her during the voyage? Or that he'd realised he didn't want to live without her? As if it was some old-fashioned scenario and he was ringing to ask her father for permission to carry on seeing her!

When the reality was that all Carlos cared about were the stupid rules—which were what the two men had colluded about in the first place. And didn't her father's words reinforce the fact that the Spaniard may have taken her to his bed, but inside he still regarded her as a spoilt little girl who needed her allowance to be doled out?

'Are you still there, Kat?'

'Yes, Daddy,' she said resignedly. 'I'm still here.'

'I just want to say…well done, darling. I'm very proud of you. The flat's all ready and you can access your bank account immediately,' he announced, and then his voice softened. 'And you can treat yourself to something nice, because I'm increasing your allowance!'

It felt a little like being offered a poisoned chalice, and the drive from the airfield left Kat feeling dejected and slightly sick.

Installed in the vast Balfour apartment which overlooked Kensington Gardens, she was soon confronted with a reality which she didn't quite understand. And at first she couldn't quite believe. Because all the signs had been there….

She'd been…

She'd felt…

She'd thought…

It was only after more reasoned consideration and a glance at the calendar that her skin began to ice, as the mixed messages which her body was sending out caused her mind to scream with confusion.

Scanning the phone book for a list of physicians, she made an appointment with a doctor and managed to get someone to see her that afternoon.

Pushing her way past the man who seemed to have been hanging around outside her apartment all week, Kat flagged down a taxi which took her straight to Harley Street and a middle-aged gynaecologist who looked at her with a frown.

'I'm not sure I understand exactly what it is you're asking me, Miss Balfour.'

'I thought I might be pregnant,' she summarised quickly. 'And then my period started. Or, at least, I thought it did. Only it hasn't, not really, not like normal. I'm not sure what's going on.'

'Let's do a couple of tests, shall we?' he questioned.

Twenty minutes later, she was in another cab heading back for the apartment, where— physically and emotionally drained—she fell into a fitful doze, and woke soon after dawn, unable to get back to sleep. She forced herself to shower and dress and spent long minutes putting on her make-up, realising how long it had been since she'd worn it. But grateful now for the mask it provided. The familiar old mask which was now back in place—something for her to hide behind. Because new and scary territory had opened up before her and she was going to have to face it. Alone.

She'd just finished dressing when the silence was broken by the loud jangling of the telephone. It was her sister Sophie, who wasn't usually given to making early morning phone calls.

'Hello, Sophie,' said Kat, trying to sound like her 'normal' self, even though she seemed to have forgotten what that felt like. 'This is a surprise.'

'Have you seen the papers?' her sister demanded.

'No. I've only just got back from...' Suddenly, Kat registered the urgency in her sister's voice. 'Why? What's happened?'

'There's a picture of you on page three of the *Daily View*. Coming out of a *doctor's surgery* in Harley Street.' Sophie's voice dropped to a worried whisper. 'Kat, are you *okay*?'

What would her shy, artistic sister say if she told her the truth? 'I'm fine,' lied Kat, as the doorbell began peeling with a loud and imperious bell. 'Listen, someone's at the door. I'd better go, Soph. I'll ring you.'

Flicking her hair away from her face, she ran to the door, peering at the CCTV image of the man who stood outside the apartment block and then freezing in disbelief.

Carlos!

Kat's knees buckled and she swayed. Thoughts which were already confused now began to go into overdrive.

Carlos?

The doorbell rang again—and it seemed that this time he must have jammed his thumb on the bell and left it there so that she was forced to click on the intercom without giving herself a chance to compose herself. Though maybe that would have been asking too much of anyone.

'Y-yes?'

'Let me in.'

'What the hell are you doing here?'

On the doorstep, Carlos failed to make the obvious response; his mood was too black for that. 'I said…*let me in.*'

Trembling, she pressed the button, dashing

into the bathroom to check her appearance—
but there was barely any time to brush her teeth
before a loud thumping on the door announced
his presence. He must have run up the stairs,
she found herself thinking inconsequentially,
because the ancient elevator took ages.

Opening the door to him, she could see
that her assumption had been correct—since
he was slightly out of breath and his colour
was raised—but most of all she noticed the
rage which sparked in dark flames from his
ebony eyes. He was carrying a newspaper in
one hand and he looked *furious*. Pushing past
her, he slammed the door shut behind him
and then turned on her.

'*Perra,*' he whispered, his face contorted
into a dark mask of anger which automatically made Kat's heart begin a frantic racing.
'You lying little cheat.' He took a deep breath
and pushed his face a little closer to hers—
but a wave of minty toothpaste hit him and
this, with the glossy fall of hair and the carefully made-up face, was enough to make him
recoil as if he'd just been bitten by a snake.
He stared at the tight, white jeans she wore
and the cute silk T-shirt—which was exactly

the same colour as the costly aquamarines which glittered at her throat. He found himself looking at the sleek and pampered little rich girl and it was as if the past few weeks simply hadn't happened.

'And there was me thinking that you'd changed,' he raged. 'That you were no longer the girl who ran away at the first opportunity. Who had learned to deal with life and look it in the face. But, no, I was wrong. Very, very wrong. First you lie to me, and then you run— just the way you've always run! Commitment?' he bit out. 'You wouldn't know the word *commitment* if it jumped out and shook you!'

Kat was trembling as the force of his words compounded her own growing sense of realisation, and fear. And with it came the sinking sensation that he was all too eager to think the worst of her. 'You've seen the paper?' she questioned.

Carlos looked as if he was about to explode. 'So you *know* about the paper? Of course I've seen the damned paper!' And then his face darkened with suspicion. 'Is this some kind of elaborate set-up?' he demanded. 'A teaser for some newspaper deal you're setting up? Have you perhaps succeeded where every other journalist has failed in "getting to know" the real Carlos Guerrero and are about to do an exposé on me?'

Kat felt sick. How could she have ever believed he felt for her anything other than contempt? The fact that he hadn't been able to keep his hands off her while she'd been on board his yacht meant nothing. *Nothing,* she reminded herself bitterly.

'We can't have this conversation here,' she said dully—for she was afraid that if she didn't sit down she might do something unforgivable. Like faint. Or be sick—a fear which now felt very real indeed.

Without waiting for his reply she began walking towards the sitting room, aware that he was following her. She turned around as he came into the room, wondering how a man could possibly dwarf a room as huge as the main drawing room of the Balfour apartment—but somehow Carlos managed it quite effortlessly. In his dark suit and snowy shirt, he looked the epitome of crisp elegance. And a complete stranger.

'I haven't seen the paper,' she said.

His eyes narrowed. 'But you knew about it?'

'My sister rang.'

'How convenient.'

'May I see it, please?'

He half threw it onto the coffee table and Kat knelt down and opened it up with hands which were shaking. And there, on page three, was the article Sophie had alerted her to.

It wasn't the first time she had been featured in a national newspaper but it was the first time she had been visibly shocked by what she saw. The Kat who had been photographed leaving the doctor's rooms in Harley Street was barely recognisable as herself. Her face looked bleached, her eyes huge and a pashmina shawl hugged around her shoulders seemed to envelope her.

But it was the headline—and the subsequent article which disturbed her far more.

Guerrero's Society Babe Visits Baby Doc.

Swallowing down her disbelief, Kat read on.

Famous ex-bullfighter Carlos Guerrero is used to playing cloak-and-dagger—

and the latest beauty in his life seems to be following in his footsteps. Fresh from a Mediterranean trip on the Spanish billionaire's luxury yacht, stunning Kat Balfour was tight-lipped as she left Dr. Steve Smith's Harley Street surgery. Dr. Smith is best known for his delivery of last year's Royal Princess and his spokesperson refused to comment on rumours that one of the notorious Balfour Babes is pregnant.

Kat Balfour hails from one of the richest and most scandal-ridden families in the land, but her new beau is more than a match for their colourful history. Playboy tycoon Guerrero was once tipped to be Spain's finest bullfighter before dramatically withdrawing from the ring, fifteen years ago.

Who knows? With capricious Kat Balfour at his side, the man tagged 'Cold Heart' by the Spanish tabloids may have taken on his biggest challenge yet!

Dazed, Kat sat back on her heels and stared up at the forbidding mask of Carlos's face.

'But they didn't ask me to comment!' she protested. 'I didn't even know they had a snapper there!'

Carlos clenched his fists in fury. 'Is that all you care about?' he demanded. 'The fact that you didn't know you were being photo-graphed? Why, would you have applied a little more gloss to those lying lips of yours?'

Her heart began to race as she registered the venom in his voice. 'How dare you speak to me like this?'

'Quite easily,' he snapped. 'And before you start to offer any half-hearted defence, surely the fundamental flaw in your argument is that you lied to me, Kat. But we could spend the whole morning railing against each other and none of it is relevant. In fact, only one thing is.' He fixed her in the piercing spotlight of his ebony eyes. 'Just tell me one thing. Are you or are you not…pregnant?'

There was a horrible pause and the only sound which Kat could register was the un-comfortable irregularity of her own breath-ing. 'I…'

'*Are* you?'

'Yes! *Yes!*'

He let out a hiss, like the sound of a pressure cooker which has just had its lid removed after many hours of being on the boil. 'So you *did* lie,' he said in a voice which sounded suddenly flat.

Kat shook her head. 'Not exactly.'

Cold black eyes were turned on her. 'Not *exactly*? How many variations of the truth are there? Perhaps you'd care to explain, or did I dream up the fact that you told me you needed to find a chemist because your period had come?'

'I thought...' Stupidly, she was blushing now. 'I got a pain during the night and I started bleeding.' The night he hadn't been there—when his absence had seemed to emphasise that there was nothing between them but an enforced captivity while they waited to discover whether or not they were going to be parents. 'I thought it was my period. It was only when I'd been home for a couple of days that I realised that it wasn't.'

'But you weren't going to bother to tell me about it?'

'Of course I was! I just needed it to be confirmed first.'

'Or was it something more than that?' he demanded, his heart beating now with a slow and steady kind of dread. 'Did you go to the doctor for something other than confirmation?'

It took a moment or two for his meaning to register and, when it did, Kat thought she really *might* be sick. Swallowing down the bile which had risen in her throat, she stared at him. 'How…how *dare* you suggest such a disgusting thing?' she spat out, trying now to rise from her subordinate position on her knees. But her rage was so intense that she half stumbled and Carlos automatically put out his hand to support her. 'Get away from me!' she flared.

He took no notice, just made sure that she was steady once more and then strode over to the window, looking out at the manicured beauty which was Kensington Gardens— seeing the glitter of the Round Pool in the distance, trying desperately to assemble his thoughts into some kind of order.

It was several moments before he had composed himself enough to turn round and, when he did, it was to see that Kat was sitting in the centre of a huge, overstuffed sofa, looking impossibly fragile. And in that moment, he could have kicked himself for the whiplash quality of his words. What kind of a brute was he, he wondered disgustedly, to harangue a woman who was newly pregnant?

'Can I get you something?' he questioned in a hollow voice. 'Something to drink?'

'I feel sick.'

Quickly, he found a bathroom at the end of one of the long corridors and tipped out a pile of rose petals which had been cluttering up a porcelain bowl and then took it to Kat. On further exploration of the apartment, he discovered a high-tech kitchen, where he made a pot of ginger-and-lemon tea, because he remembered reading somewhere that ginger was good for nausea.

She was still sitting where he'd left her, the towel on her lap, the porcelain bowl empty at her side. And suddenly he looked beyond her painted face and saw the vulnerability in her huge eyes.

'I've made you tea,' he said quickly, as he put the tray down.

She looked up, telling herself again that she must be strong. Carlos hadn't broken any promises. He'd never claimed to *feel* anything for her. She certainly couldn't demand love from him because she was carrying his baby. And she must close the floodgates on her love for him. He mustn't know about it. It wouldn't be fair—because then, wouldn't she be burdening him with unnecessary guilt as well as a baby he'd never planned?

'I didn't run away,' she told him tiredly. 'I honestly thought my period had come, so there was no reason to stay. We'd already decided that.' And he had done nothing to stop her leaving, had he? That had been the bottom line. Even now, he was only here because he *had* to be—not because he wanted to. 'But I'd just had some kind of bleeding—apparently, it's not unusual in the early stages of pregnancy.'

'But you're okay?' he demanded urgently.

'I'm okay.'

'And…the baby? The baby is okay?'

'The doctor tells me that everything's fine.'

'Thank *God*,' he breathed.

And for the first time, Carlos began to take in the enormity of what she had just told him. A single fact that had the power to change his life for ever. He was going to be a *father*. Placing a delicate mug of steaming tea into her unprotesting hand, he realised that his baby was growing beneath her heart even now—deep in her belly.

He wanted to reach out and touch her—to place the palm of his hand on her still-flat belly, as if to reassure himself that his child really was in there. But he felt as if he had forfeited the right to do any such thing, his bitter accusations driving a wedge between the two of them. And he wondered now if his father had bequeathed him something of his own cruelty—whether or not he was fit to be a father to her child.

He flinched. 'You know that there were photographers hanging around outside when I arrived and that it's only going to get worse?'

'But *why*?' she wailed, letting her hormones get the better of her. 'Why can't they just leave me alone?'

His body tensed. 'It is the joint legacy we share, *Princesa*. One which is bread and meat to the ever-hungry media,' he said bitterly. 'The ex-matador and his scandalous heiress.'

At that moment the telephone began to

shrill and, putting her tea down on the table, Kat leaned over and picked it up. It was her father.

'Would you mind telling me what the hell is going on, Kat?' he began ominously.

Kat opened her mouth to start explaining when it suddenly hit her that she didn't *have to*. She didn't have to do anything. Not any more. Maybe in the past she *had* run away from her responsibilities—and maybe her father's set of Rules had helped her see her life in a different light. Or maybe Carlos had. But she wasn't running now. Even if she wanted to—which she didn't—running was no longer an option. She was going to be a mother. She was going to have Carlos's baby and she was going to have to learn to stand on her own two feet. And that meant that the rest of the Balfours were really going to have to butt out and leave her to get on with it.

Without thinking about it, her fingers of one hand drifted to her stomach and she let them rest there—almost protectively—looking up to see a sudden flare of light in the ebony eyes which were fixed on her.

She turned her lips back to the mouthpiece.

'Actually, I don't really want to talk to anyone at the moment, Daddy,' she said steadily.

'But—'

'No buts. I'm fine.' She listened to her father for a minute, acutely aware of Carlos's intense scrutiny. 'Yes, he's here. With me. No, Daddy. No. I'll talk to you in a couple of days. Yes. I promise.'

Slowly, she replaced the receiver and Carlos saw the wariness in her eyes as she regarded him—as if expecting him to start interrogating her again. His mouth hardened. And maybe she had good reason to think that.

The phone began to ring once more and, seeing her eyes close wearily this time, Carlos snatched up the receiver, his eyes narrowing as he listened. 'Yes?'

'Carlos! It's Tania Stephens here,' came the throaty voice of a woman. 'I'm the one who left my bikini on your yacht and wondered if you'd just like to—'

'No comment,' he snarled, slamming it down again, and when it began to ring again almost immediately he took it off the hook. Was this what it was going to be like? he wondered. With the phone ringing and the press clamouring and Kat getting bigger. Living out her pregnancy in the middle of the city, with that cold and unapproachable air about her while the media-hungry world closed in.

There was a solution to the problem which lay before them, he realised slowly. But only if Kat would agree to it—and that was by no means certain. 'I can find you somewhere safe to stay,' he said slowly. 'Somewhere the press won't bother you.'

She looked up. 'Where?'

'That's up to you, *Princesa*. I can give you several options. I have places pretty much all over the world you can choose from.'

'With you, you mean? You'll be coming with me?' she questioned in a cool voice, as if she didn't care one way or the other. Because the last thing she wanted or needed to feel right now was disappointment when he told her that, no, he'd be leaving her alone to face the coming months.

Carlos expelled a breath. 'Well, that depends,' he said slowly. 'On whether or not you want me there.'

There was a pause while the question hung in the air.

Don't make yourself vulnerable, Kat told herself. Don't open yourself up to yet more pain. 'If you want,' she said, with a shrug. 'I don't really care either way.'

Carlos met the blue of her dazzling eyes which now seemed as cold as a winter sky. She had agreed to leave the spotlight of the city and he was going with her.

His mouth hardened. It may have felt a little like a victory, he thought, but it seemed a very hollow one.

CHAPTER TWELVE

HE TOOK her to a house she recognised, though it took a moment or two for Kat to realise why.

'It's the house in the painting!' she exclaimed, her heart lifting with an unexpected kind of delight. 'The one in your study on the yacht.' The one she used to gaze at when she was transcribing recipes during a time which now seemed like light years ago.

'It is indeed. My hacienda,' said Carlos softly.

Standing in the doorway of the lovingly cared-for old house, surrounded by a shaded veranda decked with flowers and foliage, Kat looked out at the stunning Andalusian countryside. Outside were orchards of Carlos's very own oranges and lemons—which scented the soft, warm air. And in nearby pastures overlooking distant mountain peaks lived his beloved Andalusian horses which people came from all over the world to buy.

Despite her mixed emotions, Kat thought she had never seen anywhere more lovely in her life. It seemed so solid and real—so far away from the hustle and bustle of the city. And it made her feel indescribably wistful for a life she had never known and probably never would. A life with deep roots and the promise of longevity.

'So what do you think of my home?' asked Carlos, as he came out of the house to find her standing there, perfectly still. They'd travelled down earlier that afternoon on the jet he'd hired, and Kat had just drunk tea and eaten from a dish of fruit which his house-keeper had served to them.

She turned to face him. 'I think it's beautiful.'

'So why the troubled look?'

Was he completely dense, Kat wondered, or did he just have the ability to completely switch off? Maybe with men it was different—or maybe it was just different for Carlos.

Beneath her outwardly calm exterior she could feel the riot of emotions which were as tangled as an old ball of string, but presumably he suffered no similar disquiet as he contemplated their uncertain future.

'Oh, it's all been a lot to take in,' she said evasively. 'The news about the baby, the journey here—wondering just what we're going to tell people.' She bit her lip. Plus the mind-boggling adjustment of having to redefine herself as a single mother. 'And when.'

Staring down into her bright blue eyes, Carlos saw the unmistakable strain which shadowed them. And wondered whether the brittleness she seemed to have acquired might melt away again. So that once again she became that soft, smiling Kat who used to tease him. The woman who used to welcome him into her arms and into her bed every night.

'We're not going to do anything until you've relaxed,' he said softly. 'That was one of my reasons for bringing you here.'

Not quite daring to ask him what any of the others were, Kat returned his stare. 'And what about you, Carlos—what will you be doing? Relaxing—or tapping away on your damned computer as usual?'

He heard something which sounded close to accusation in her voice and Carlos nodded. 'I think I might try a little relaxation therapy myself,' he agreed softly. 'There happens to be a pool here which I haven't swum in this year.'

There was indeed a pool—and Kat blinked with disbelief when she first saw it. A vast infinity pool overlooking an enormous mountain range, the clear blue waters seeming to go on for ever.

After breakfast the following morning, he suggested she change into a swimsuit and meet him there. And although it was a sensible enough suggestion for such a sunny day it seemed a curiously *intimate* thing to say. Lazing by a swimming pool was the sort of thing which couples did and they were most definitely not a couple—a state of affairs which had been reinforced by the fact that they'd spent their first night at the hacienda sleeping in separate rooms.

Well, of *course they had.* Carlos wasn't interested in her any more, was he? Not in that way.

Because he hadn't touched her. Not once.

Not a tight, comforting hug when she'd told him about the baby. Not a squeeze of her fingers during the flight over here, nor even a protective hand held at the small of her back as he guided her through the doors of his beloved hacienda for the first time.

Nothing.

And didn't that send out the clearest message of all—that the sexual side of their relationship was over? That really, everything between them was over—other than the mechanics of working out how to manage their shared parenthood. She guessed that at some point they were going to have to sit down and discuss what the future was going to bring, but she knew without him having to tell her that it was not going to include coupledom.

Kat went to her room and changed into a bikini which seemed too skimpy for comfort—though, logically, she knew that her body had not yet begun to alter. Just that now it felt more vulnerable than it used to. More exposed. Just like she did. Pulling on a silken robe and carrying a book she had little enthusiasm for, she went downstairs to find Carlos was already by the pool.

He looked up as she approached, and frowned. 'You need a hat.'

'I haven't brought one with me.'

'Well, there are plenty around the place. Here. Have this.'

Fishing out a battered old panama from underneath one of the loungers, he tossed it to her, and she caught it.

'Thanks.' Her throat was dry as she slipped off her silken robe and lay down beside him. It was still early and the air was fresh and sweet. Unknown birds were making distant calls and she could smell the heavy fragrance of jasmine.

For a while she felt brittle, unsure of what to do or say to the man whose golden-olive body was so near—and yet which might as well have been on a distant planet for all the closeness which existed between them. There were a million things she felt she should ask him, but she was too weary to begin, and the sun sinking into her skin was so very distracting…and gradually it made her relax a little. She drank some cool water and picked up her book. Put it down again, and dozed.

Deep, accented words floated into her

dreamless state and she looked up to find that Carlos was leaning over her, his black eyes gleaming with concern. 'You'll burn if you're not careful,' he said softly. 'Want me to rub some cream on for you?'

'I...' What could she say? That she was afraid if he touched her she might not be able to control her emotions, or her body's response to him? She would risk burning her skin because she was so vulnerable around him? How pathetic was that? Kat nodded, tongue flicking out over suddenly bone-dry lips. 'If you don't mind.'

Mind? Carlos's mouth hardened. 'Turn over.' He squeezed lotion onto the firm flesh between her shoulder blades and then began to rub it in, expelling a slow rush of air as he felt the silken texture of her skin beneath his fingers. How long had it been since he had touched her like this? Pushing aside the straps of her bikini he began to massage her tight muscles, feeling some of the tension begin to melt beneath his questing fingers.

'Carlos...'

'Is that good, *Princesa*?'

Squeezing her eyes tightly shut, Kat

couldn't make up her mind whether she wanted to laugh or cry. 'Well, yes…yes, it's good.' Of course it was good.

'Then lie back and enjoy it.'

Was he *mad*? Didn't he realise that, with his hands edging down to the wide band of flesh which lay above her bikini bottom, she just wanted to wriggle and squirm and pull him down against her rapidly warming body? Against her and into her. To feel his hard flesh united with hers once again. Kat swallowed. Now his fingers were kneading at the tops of her thighs—and this was really dangerous territory because what else would account for her almost strangled little gulp and the terrible sexual hunger which had begun to bubble up inside her?

'Carlos!' she said urgently.

'What? What is it, *Princesa*?'

'I…I…'

And suddenly Carlos couldn't bear it for a second longer, knowing that he was about to fall into a snare of his own making. Knowing full well that he could seduce her in an instant, exactly where she was. He wouldn't even have to meet the expression in her cold, hurt eyes. Could thrust into her from behind for a wordless and blissful coupling, knowing that they would both gasp out their relieved fulfilment and then it would be over. Their frustration forgotten and their bodies satisfied. And suddenly registering the certainty that it was no longer enough. Not nearly enough. Not any more.

Yes, it would be as easy as breathing to take her, but where would that leave them? Hadn't he used the power of his sexual expertise to shield him from life for too long, seeking the heady power of sex as a substitute for emotion, time after time? And didn't he owe this woman the truth, no matter how hard it was for him to admit it?

Turning her over, he stared down into her face—at the dark dilation of her blue eyes and the flare of colour which washed across her cheekbones—and felt a strange rush of something like pain in his heart. He had faced death and danger many times during his life, but he had never known such a feeling of trepidation. How was it possible to face the mighty wrath of a thirteen-hundred-pound animal in the bullring with a degree of steadfastness and resolve…and yet be rendered weak by the blaze in a woman's beautiful blue eyes?

'I'm sorry,' he said simply.

Kat frowned. What was he saying—that he'd changed his mind about making love to her when it had obviously been on his mind only seconds ago? 'Sorry?' she echoed. 'What for?'

He gave a bitter laugh. 'How long have you got? For doubting you. For being a victim of my own prejudice. For not realising that the woman I saw on my boat was the real you, not the poor little rich girl I was determined to see. That once you'd peeled away the layers you'd used to protect yourself from the tough blows that life had dealt you, I caught a glimpse of the woman you really were. The real Kat. That beneath all the finery was something much more precious.' For a moment his voice sounded shaken. 'And that something was you.'

Kat stared at him, confusion tempered with the frantic clamour of her mind telling her not to raise her hopes. Not to let him hurt her. Not any more. 'Are you saying all this because I'm having a baby?' she whispered.

He shook his head. 'I'm saying it because I mean it. Because I've been a fool, Kat. A stupid fool.' Taking a deep breath, he forced himself to admit why. 'Resenting you for the fact that, for the first time in my life, I lost control when I was around you. Without realising that sometimes a man needs to lose control, because that is what makes him human. What enables him to grab at the things which make life worth living.'

Suddenly, Kat could see how Carlos's steely self-will had protected *him* in exactly the same way as the armoury of her clothes and rebellious attitude had protected *her.* The two of them had a lot more in common than she'd ever realised. They'd both witnessed violence and pain. Had both deployed their own methods of coping with them.

And now?

They could, she realised, put all their demons in the past—but only if he wanted to. Because she realised something else too. That time after time she had given herself to Carlos, only to have him push her away. She understood why he had done it—but she couldn't keep on doing it. Giving was a two-way street—or there could be no true equality. No real relationship. Her voice was gentle. 'Carlos, what exactly are you saying?'

He was intelligent enough to know that this was one of life's big questions, the sort that your entire future would depend on. And even as she asked it, the answer came to him instantly, with a kind of blinding certainty he'd never before realised he was capable of.

He stared straight into her face. 'That I love you,' he said simply.

They were words she never thought she'd hear—never from Carlos—but it didn't occur to Kat to doubt them. Not for a minute. Perhaps because she sensed how much it had taken for him to say them—and because although his words could sometimes wound, they were always truthful. And perhaps because she knew that he had missed out on love for so much of his life, it didn't occur to her to hesitate. Nor to hold back in any way. In fact, she couldn't have done—for the joy in her heart was too insistent to be silenced.

'Oh, Carlos. My sweet, darling Carlos. I love you too,' she whispered. 'So much.'

He took her face in his hands, cupping its

heart shape between both palms. 'I want to marry you, Kat,' he said unsteadily. 'I want us to make a life for ourselves together. A new life. A proper life.'

And now she *did* hesitate. For Kat hadn't grown up with the best role models in the world where marriage was concerned. Her family was littered with divorces and their complicated consequences.

'And I want to be a good father,' he continued fiercely, before she had spoken. 'The best father in the world to our child. He—or she—will have their own destiny and never will I try to live my life through them.'

She heard the resolve which had deepened his voice and knew that Carlos was determined never to replicate the cruelty practised by his father. And that determination of his spurred her on. Because wasn't marriage a leap of faith for everyone? In a way, she and Carlos were lucky. They had witnessed the mistakes that other people could make with their lives—and they could do their best to ensure they didn't repeat them.'

She drew back a little as she looked up into his face. 'Oh, Carlos—of course I'll marry you. I want to marry you more than anything else on earth.'

He nodded, and for a moment there was a lump in his throat so big that he had difficulty in speaking. 'Then seal it with a kiss, *Princesa*,' he commanded at last.

Something in his eyes made her tremble and something in the sweet restorative power of his lips made her tremble even more. She sighed when he lifted her off the sunbed and carried her to the nearby cabana, where he peeled off her little lemon bikini with a quiet and urgent hunger which was underpinned with an unmistakable sense of awe.

A shaft of pure love shot through her as he positioned his powerful naked body over hers and when he filled her with one slick, long thrust, she cried out her pleasure. As sunlight and birdsong drifted in to mingle with the sound of their muffled moans of pleasure, Kat thought she had never known happiness like it.

Please make it last, she prayed silently, as she held him, both still shuddering from the sweet onslaught of their passion. But somehow she knew that they would *make* it last. The two of them—and then, one day in the coming months, three. They would do everything in their power to ensure that life would be good.

Snuggling against him, Kat felt the slowing of his heart and she nuzzled against his neck, wanting to shower him with tiny kisses which demonstrated all the love she was bursting to give him.

Funny, really—her father had sent her away to learn commitment and she had found it. It had been a tough lesson but she knuckled down to it—and Carlos had helped show her how. So really, it made sense for him to reap the benefits.

For wasn't marriage the biggest and most wonderful commitment of all?